"We can't do this,"

Phil rasped. "I must have been crazy to even consider it," he added, the words muffled against her hair.

For several seconds, Crista didn't understand. "Can't do what?" she asked in confusion, raising her face to his.

"Make love to each other." With a wrench of regret, he withdrew his hands from beneath her sweater. She was so soft, so sensually captivating. But he knew all too well where duty lay.

"You mean...because I'm a virgin?" she asked.

"Of course, that's what I mean!" Distractedly he ran his fingers through his hair. She wasn't making this any easier.

Crista couldn't believe her ears. At long last she'd offered herself to a man, and he'd refused her because of her innocence. "I don't want your gentlemanly consideration! I'm not some sort of freak!"

"Crista...I didn't mean to imply anything like that. Can't we talk about it?" he asked her as she headed for the door.

His only answer was the heavy front door slamming resoundingly in his face. *Women!*

Dear Reader:

All of us here at Silhouette Books hope that you are having a wonderful summer, and enjoying all that the season has to offer. Whether you are vacationing, or spending the long, warm summer evenings at home, we wish you the best—and hope to bring you many happy hours of romance.

August finds our DIAMOND JUBILEE in full swing. This month features *Virgin Territory* by Suzanne Carey, a delightful story about a heroine who laments being what she considers "the last virgin in Chicago." Her handsome hero feels he's a man with a mission—to protect her virtue *and* his beloved bachelorhood at the same time. Then, in September, we have an extraspecial surprise—*two* DIAMOND JUBILEE titles by two of your favorite authors: Annette Broadrick with *Married?!* and Dixie Browning with *The Homing Instinct*.

The DIAMOND JUBILEE—Silhouette Romance's tenth anniversary celebration—is our way of saying thanks to you, our readers. To symbolize the timelessness of love, as well as the modern gift of the tenth anniversary, we're presenting readers with a DIAMOND JUBILEE Silhouette Romance each month, penned by one of your favorite Silhouette Romance authors.

And that's not all! This month don't miss Diana Palmer's fortieth story for Silhouette—*Connal*. He's a LONG, TALL TEXAN out to lasso your heart! In addition, back by popular demand, are Books 4, 5 and 6 of DIANA PALMER DUETS—some of Diana Palmer's earlier published work which has been unavailable for years.

During our tenth anniversary, the spirit of celebration is with us year-round. And that's all due to you, our readers. With the support you've given us, you can look forward to many more years of heartwarming, poignant love stories.

I hope you'll enjoy this book and all of the stories to come. Come home to romance—Silhouette Romance—for always!

Sincerely,

Tara Hughes Gavin
Senior Editor

SUZANNE CAREY

Virgin Territory

Published by Silhouette Books New York

America's Publisher of Contemporary Romance

For Bonnie:
stepmother, friend and traveling companion.
Here's to the fun
we had in the Virgin Islands!

SILHOUETTE BOOKS
300 E. 42nd St., New York, N.Y. 10017

Copyright © 1990 by Verna Carey

All rights reserved. Except for use in any review, the reproduction or utilization of this work in whole or in part in any form by any electronic, mechanical or other means, now known or hereafter invented, including xerography, photocopying and recording, or in any information storage or retrieval system, is forbidden without the permission of Silhouette Books, 300 E. 42nd St., New York, N.Y. 10017

ISBN: 0-373-08736-5

First Silhouette Books printing August 1990

All the characters in this book are fictitious. Any resemblance to actual persons, living or dead, is purely coincidental.

®: Trademark used under license and registered in the United States Patent and Trademark Office and in other countries.

Printed in the U.S.A.

Books by Suzanne Carey

Silhouette Desire

Kiss and Tell #4
Passion's Portrait #69
Mountain Memory #92
Leave Me Never #126
Counterparts #176
Angel in His Arms #206
Confess to Apollo #268
Love Medicine #310
Any Pirate in a Storm #368

Silhouette Romance

A Most Convenient Marriage #633
Run Isabella #682
Virgin Territory #736

Silhouette Intimate Moments

Never Say Goodbye #330

SUZANNE CAREY

is a former reporter and magazine editor who prefers to write romance novels because they add to the sum total of love in the world.

A Note From The Author:

Dear Reader,

I've been fond of love stories ever since I can remember. In high school, I wrote (in longhand!) a romantic serial, illustrating each chapter with poster paints. Looking back, I realize it was pretty amateurish. But my friends liked it. They couldn't wait for the next installment!

Maybe it's because of my lifelong love affair with stories about men and women who grow to need and care for each other that I see the 1990 Diamond Jubilee of Silhouette Romance as such a significant event. I'm honored that this book was chosen as a Diamond Jubilee edition.

Silhouette Romance novels promise a bit of spice, a mental treat, a relaxing break in the rushed, sometimes hectic schedule of one's day. But, in my opinion, they offer a great deal more than that. Woven through each story is the strong affirmation that—even in today's world—genuine love and commitment exist.

I enjoy writing them because the problems their heros and heroines face are thoroughly contemporary. They're *our* problems, the issues that surface in our friends' lives and our daily newspaper. Yet the traditional values we continue to prize are held dear.

Like you, I enjoy reading them because they bring me home again. Each book reestablishes a cherished territory of the heart.

Sincerely,

Suzanne Carey

Chapter One

"Let go of me this minute!"

Jammed into the far corner of the luxurious passenger seat in Tony Ludlow's new Jaguar, Crista O'Malley was fighting tooth and nail for her virtue. She was also struggling for breath. Reeking of bourbon, Tony's mouth crushed hers as he tried to slip one hand beneath her skirt.

Desperately prying his fingers loose, Crista tried to evade their grasp. But she feared it was a losing battle. More than six feet tall, at least a hundred pounds heavier than she and in peak condition from regular workouts at the gym, Tony had no difficulty maintaining the upper hand.

He was also slightly inebriated. "Relax, Crista-baby," he coaxed, groping at her breasts through the protective layers of her clothing with all the subtlety of an orangutan. "I know it's awkward in the car. Too bad your roommate isn't working tonight. But there's always my apartment...."

Seemingly possessed of more limbs than a whole treeful of monkeys, he pushed up the hem of her skirt again. It was definitely time for drastic measures. Should she extricate herself with a knee to the groin the way her roommate's boyfriend had taught her? Or try to wrest the car door open and yell for the police?

She fervently hoped neither course of action would be necessary. Badly as he was behaving at the moment, Tony was an okay sort. She didn't want to cause him physical pain. As for the police, even if she didn't swear out a complaint, the incident would tarnish his reputation. One of Cook County's most promising young defense attorneys, he couldn't afford to be the butt of salacious gossip. If she knew them, the cops and their allies—Tony's opposite numbers at the state attorney's office—would be only too delighted to spread a juicy rumor about him.

Maybe she should disarm him with The Announcement. The most civilized of her available options, it didn't work well with confirmed boors or all-out mashers. But it usually did the trick where basically decent guys like Tony were concerned.

Unfortunately, as one of the Chicago *Tribune*'s felony-court reporters, she spent as much time at the courthouse as Tony did. If he was inclined to tell tales out of school, people would be whispering about her instead.

"Tony... Please!" she begged again. But the message didn't seem to be getting through.

Moments later she felt one of her nylon stockings give way as he popped open the left front fastener of her garter belt. "You don't understand!" she blurted. "I've never made love to a man."

As if their entire wrestling match existed solely on videotape and someone had pushed the Stop button, Tony froze. "You're kidding, right?" he asked with a worried frown. "I thought you told me you were twenty-six."

Clearly, The Announcement had produced a sobering effect. Sitting up, Crista tucked her tweed skirt primly about her knees. "I *am* twenty-six," she answered. "What does that have to do with anything?"

"Well, I just thought..."

Straightening his tie, Tony eased back behind the wheel and broke open a pack of chewing gum. For the time since she'd known him, her smooth-talking date was at a loss for words.

No doubt he thinks there's something wrong with me, Crista acknowledged as she tidied her mahogany-dark page boy into place. If I haven't slept with somebody by this ripe old age, I must be frigid. Or neurotic. Maybe both.

Why was it nobody ever guessed her true motive—the old-fashioned conviction that she should save her virginity for the man she would marry someday?

The way things are going, she thought, I'll never get to *know* any man well enough to marry him. I don't love Tony, and after what happened tonight, I probably never could. But he's a nice enough guy compared to some I've known. When he found out what the situation was, he didn't keep pressuring me. I'll bet if I asked him to make love to me now, he'd refuse.

"Listen, Crista..." he muttered with an obvious attempt to ease the strain between them. "I feel like a real chump about this. But I swear to God I never dreamed..."

"What if you had?"

Would you have invited me out in the first place? she asked him silently. Or would you have gone foraging in greener pastures? Must every casual friendship between a man and woman lead to bed?

"I...uh...don't know." Her question seemed to make Tony more uncomfortable than ever. "One thing's certain," he admitted. "I'm glad you told me. If I'd known, I'd never have tried to jump your bones the way I did."

For Crista, the slang expression said it all. In her opinion, the impersonal act of "jumping someone's bones" had to be light-years removed from genuine lovemaking. But even if she were willing to jettison her principles and have sex outside of marriage with someone she loved, how was she supposed to get from point A—mere acquaintance—to point B—a love relationship—? Every guy she met expected her to go to bed by the third date!

"Maybe I should go up," she said with a sigh. "Tomorrow's the first day of the *Mercer-Watkins* trial and..."

"Judge Byrne is going to continue that case." The moment the words passed his lips, Tony acted as if he'd like to recall them. He probably supposed she'd use them as an excuse to draw out their conversation.

Don't worry, Crista thought. I don't have the slightest intention of prolonging this misery for a single moment. "In any case, tomorrow is Monday," she went on smoothly, picking up her purse. "I like to get an early start."

He gave her a grateful look. "I'll walk you to the door."

The apartment Crista shared with assistant copy editor Laurin Hayes was on the third floor of a six-unit buff brick building several blocks west of the lake and Lincoln Park. The neighborhood was a good one by Chicago standards, but the hour was late and Crista was grateful for Tony's reassuring presence as she fumbled for the key.

"Thanks, umm, for a lovely time," she murmured out of habit before she could stop herself.

If Tony rolled his eyes heavenward at the impossible irony of the cliché, she wasn't aware of it. "No problem," he responded amiably, not offering to kiss her goodnight. "I'll call you sometime next week, okay?"

"Fine," she answered, knowing it was a promise he wouldn't keep. She didn't need the John Hancock building to fall on her head in order to recognize a brush-off.

Laurin and her significant other, Dan Curran, were nibbling cold pizza and watching late-night television when she entered the apartment. "What's up?" Dan asked, taking a long, hard look at her face. A sportswriter who also worked at the *Tribune*, he was extremely observant and seldom minced words.

Crista shrugged. For the first time since the onset of her confrontation with Tony, she wanted to cry. Though she didn't mind losing him as an escort, the pattern was getting to be all too familiar. And that familiarity was beginning to hurt. Something similar had happened to her several months earlier with a man she'd really cared about.

Another lawyer she'd met at the courthouse, Greg Maas had seemed so mature, so understanding. Far from appearing turned off by her stance, he'd expressed his admiration. They'd continued to see each other, spending many pleasant evenings together. She'd actually begun to congratulate herself that adherence to principle had paid off, when he'd swept the rug out from under her feet.

Next month Greg would marry another woman he'd been dating while he was seeing her. His bride-to-be, an experienced twenty-two-year-old, hadn't been too principled for an occasional roll in the hay. Despite their differing views in some areas, Greg was a real catch and Crista had been the loser. Or so it seemed to her.

"What's usually up when I come in with my clothes all mussed and my ego in shreds?" she rejoined with a sniff.

"Not again!" Laurin, a thirty-two-year-old divorcée from Atlanta who spoke in dulcet Southern tones gave

Crista a sympathetic look. "I *am* sorry," she said. "Your friend Tony seemed so nice...."

"He is nice. We agreed to disagree about values, that's all." Shrugging off her coat, Crista curled up dejectedly on the sofa opposite her friends. "Sometimes I think the whole struggle is wasted effort," she continued after a moment, noting the comfortable way Dan's palm rested on Laurin's blue-jeans-clad thigh. "Maybe I should just sleep with someone and get it over with."

In his untidy and fiercely private corner of the *Tribune*'s feature department, Phil Catterini was staring at a blank computer screen. Several mugs partially filled with stale coffee were ranged on the desktop. In one of them a healthy culture of mold had started to grow. The sky outside his window was opaque and leaden with the promise of snow.

Actually, he consoled himself, the computer screen wasn't completely blank. Half an hour earlier, he'd entered his byline and the appropriate slug for his thrice-weekly column, "Catbird Seat," carefully coding the words for boldface type. It was his *mind* that was genuinely empty—utterly devoid of worthwhile and/or entertaining topics. He considered booking a one-way flight to Vail and learning to live as a ski bum. Or going back to work as an ace reporter for the city desk. At least with a police radio sputtering at his elbow, a man knew he'd have something to write about.

Hell, he thought, curiously inspecting the mold culture through owlish reading glasses. I can't complain. Another Royko, some of the media critics were calling him— and talking syndication. It was heady stuff.

Unfortunately so much attention was forcing him to keep his standards high. Any old snow job just wouldn't make the grade these days. His public—and that included his colleagues on the *Tribune*'s editorial staff—expected a lot of him. They wanted something insouciant, thought-provoking and mildly outrageous with their morning coffee. And he was fresh out of that particular commodity at the moment.

Idly he reread the note left in his mailbox by a young female reporter from city side. Though he'd never exchanged two words with her, she'd written to tell him how much she'd enjoyed a recent effort of his. "Keep up the good work," she'd scrawled in her rounded, girlish hand. I'll be damned if I can do it this morning, he thought.

His sense of malaise only increased when he tried to decide if he missed Irene Maher, the latest in a long line of "fiancées" he'd presented to his family with absolutely no thought of marriage in mind. There'd been a card from Irene in the morning mail, stamped with the postmark of a war-torn Central American country. She'd been gone on special assignment for nearly three months now, in the company of a male photographer he liked but didn't trust. And Phil was getting restless. Though he didn't love Irene any more than he had her predecessors, she gave a certain focus to his life. Yet, even before her departure he'd realized something was missing from their relationship—some elusive but profound quality he couldn't quite articulate.

"Waiting for inspiration to strike?" With his usual wry grin, Dan Curran perched on the edge of Phil's desk, occupying the only spot that wasn't piled several inches high with books and papers. "When are you gonna clean out those coffee cups?" he demanded.

"When I get a decent idea for tomorrow's column, dammit." Despite his irritable scowl, Phil knew Dan wouldn't take offense. The sportswriter knew him well; they went back a long way.

Dan gave him a speculative look. "Could be I've got one for you," he said.

"So? Let's hear it." Leaning back in his chair, Phil propped up his feet on a stack of mail.

For some reason, Dan appeared to hesitate. "You've got to promise me the girl I'm going to tell you about will remain anonymous," he said. "Otherwise..."

A frown drew Phil's emphatic dark brows together. "You know I can't guarantee anything like that until you tell me what the story's about," he answered, running his fingers through stylishly cut but unkempt dark hair in a characteristic gesture.

Dan regarded his friend's aquiline nose, firmly chiseled mouth and stubborn jaw for a moment without speaking. "She's kind of special," he said. "I wouldn't want her to get hurt."

Though Phil didn't like giving in, this time he didn't have much choice. In Dan's own quiet way, he seemed adamant. Meanwhile Phil didn't possess even the germ of a topic. To make matters worse, he was a slow and careful writer—one who agonized over every word and polished each phrase within an inch of its life. Of course, he had until the following morning at ten to produce his latest opus. But he recognized writer's block when he saw it. And without a topic or an issue to get his creative juices flowing again, tomorrow's deadline would discover him twisting in the wind.

"Okay, you win," he conceded brusquely. "Tell me about this girl."

Crista looked up to see Phil Catterini crossing the newsroom in her general direction. What he's doing over here? she wondered. Slumming? Her boss, Harry Jenkins, Phil's former editor and one of the few people Phil stopped to chat with on the city staff, wasn't in at the moment.

She had to admit Phil was a good-looking man. Not my type, of course, she added hastily, lowering her gaze to a nearly completed news feature she was writing about courthouse nepotism. But handsome in a pugnacious, street-smart sort of way. Too bad he believes his own publicity. The note she'd sent him praising a recent column had gone unanswered. He hadn't accorded her a wave or a grin, let alone a modest word of thanks.

To her consternation, Phil halted in front of her desk. "Crista O'Malley?" he asked on a tentative note.

Thunderstruck, she nodded. Seen close up, his eyes were a clear, light hazel with golden glints in them, like some powerful jungle animal's. This man is no orangutan, she thought, unable to keep from comparing him with Tony. He's a full-fledged, woman-eating tiger.

To her surprise, he seemed oddly diffident, as if he expected to suffer some sort of rebuff at her hands.

"I'm Phil Catterini," he said, stating what he must surely know was the obvious. He had a broad Chicago accent that stemmed from his upbringing in a predominantly Italian neighborhood. The timbre of his voice had the quality of rough velvet. "Though we haven't met, I'm familiar with your byline," he added. "Dan Curran suggested I talk with you."

He held out his hand.

Surrendering hers, Crista didn't speak. In point of fact, she couldn't. The physical contact had generated a warm, tingling sensation that was like a mild electrical shock. She could feel it spreading from her fingertips to her toes, suggesting the most outrageous possibilities.

"Dan thought you might be an apt subject for my column," he continued, apparently unaffected. "Mind if I pull up a chair?"

What in the world makes him think people would want to read about *me*? Crista wondered, willing herself to indifference. He and Dan must have been talking about some aspect of the courthouse beat. Well, whatever the paper's star columnist wanted, she wasn't surprised to learn he had an ulterior motive for introducing himself to her.

"Suit yourself," she answered shortly, turning back to the block of text on her computer screen. "This feature is due at noon and I have to finish it. What do you want to know?"

"I'm not sure where to start."

Phil Catterini, the tough kid from the West Side who had knocked everybody's socks off as a crime reporter, unsure of himself? Phil Catterini, whose smashing "Catbird Seat" column was about to be syndicated? Would wonders never cease?

"Try the beginning," Crista said.

His mouth curved at last, as if he was suddenly seeing her as a person and not just as a potential source.

Phil studied her face for a few seconds. He found her petite and just shy of pretty, with good bone structure and a nice figure. She had curves in all the right places. Her best features were big green eyes that spoke eloquently of her considerable intelligence, and a shining cap of thick, dark hair with reddish highlights. The lively sparkle in her eyes and the intrinsic glow of her cheeks and hair brought to mind words like *healthy* and *natural*. She wore very little makeup.

She's the kind of woman a man wants to nurture and protect, Phil said to himself absently.

A moment later he was startled by his own reaction. Protection was probably the last thing Crista O'Malley needed. She seemed like a very self-possessed young woman—one who must have quite a bit going for her if Harry had assigned her to that zoo of a courthouse. She did a damn good job of covering it, too. Last week's story about that bizarre murder case had been right on target.

Yet despite Crista's obvious tough-mindedness when it came to her work, he knew he hadn't been wrong about her vulnerability. All this remarkably fresh-faced young woman wants is to get married and let the man of her choice be the first to make mad, passionate love to her, he thought. As a goal it's admirable. And probably doomed.

Typing half a sentence and then deleting it, Crista tried not to squirm beneath the luminous intensity of his gaze. She was determined not to let him see how attracted she felt. "Well?" she asked impatiently, arching delicate brows.

"Dan tells me you claim to be the last twenty-six-year-old virgin in Chicago," he answered. "And that you're considering throwing in the towel."

He was nothing if not direct. Crista gave him a stricken look. As if someone had turned up the dial on her body's thermostat, she blushed a rosy pink from the roots of her hair to the vanishing point of her neckline. Heat flooded through her in waves.

"How *dare* Dan betray a confidence like that?" she raged when finally she could speak. "And to an absolute stranger!"

For some reason, her characterization of him as a stranger set Phil on his ear. So what if they hadn't met before? They worked for the same newspaper, didn't they?

"I wouldn't say he did that, exactly...."

Reproached by the mute rejoinder in her anguished green eyes, Phil shook his head in frustration. "Oh, hell," he admitted. "I suppose he did. But he made me promise to keep your name out of it if you agreed to talk to me."

"And if I don't? I suppose you'll feel free to broadcast my predicament all over the newsroom!"

By now, several of the other reporters were staring at them and Crista wished she hadn't raised her voice. Phil had done nothing to deserve that kind of tongue-lashing and she knew it. Offered a tip that might lead to a good story, she'd have followed up on it herself. But the issue was a highly personal one. And despite all the sensitive stories she'd written about other people, she didn't like being on the other side of the notebook.

Phil was looking annoyed, too. "I hope you realize I wouldn't do anything like that," he said.

"Maybe I do." Feeling slightly ashamed of herself, she faced him with determination. "I don't want to be in your column," she whispered. "Not even anonymously. Please don't ask me again."

She didn't really expect him to give up without a fight.

"Look," he persisted. "I can imagine how you feel. But nobody will guess it's you. The clash of old and new morality is a valid issue. If I told your story in the column, it would be like taking a survey. Should you or shouldn't you? People would write in with their opinions. They'd help you decide."

Such an idea had never occurred to her. Briefly Crista wavered, torn between her deep need for privacy and her curiosity about the kind of advice she might get. For some reason she hated to disappoint this persuasive tiger of a man who pled his case in loosened tie, rolled-up shirt-sleeves and faded jeans.

The need for privacy won out. "My answer is *no*," she said, turning back to her video display terminal with a vengeance. "If you'll forgive me, Mr. Catterini, I've got work to do."

Though it had never occurred before, she ran into Phil at lunch. Something told her it wasn't by happenstance. The little hangout across from the paper was crammed with reporters, editors and advertising types. In that impatient crush, he had managed somehow to secure a stool next to hers.

"Corned beef on rye," she ordered, resolutely keeping her profile turned to him as she braced herself for another argument. "And diet cola. Hold the fries."

Phil ogled her as if they were the sparring halves of an otherwise loving couple. "I'll have a hero on Italian bread with plenty of mustard and mayo," he said. "A double order of fries. And coffee with cream and sugar. I guess that's it."

Unaccountably, his proximity was doing curious things to Crista's breathing. She felt hyperaware of his broad shoulders, crisp, dark hair and muscular forearms. He had large, capable-looking hands, and she wondered if they were gentle when he was making love.

Glaring at him for calling forth such totally unacceptable fantasies, she turned to the waitress. "Please...see that we get separate checks."

"Nonsense," he interjected calmly. "I'm buying today, sweetheart."

The overworked server merely shrugged and threw Phil an appreciative look as she hurried off to place their orders. "I'll just have to pay you then, *darling*," Crista told him ungraciously. "I have no intention of changing my mind about the column. Or letting you buy me lunch."

His coffee and her cola arrived and they sipped in silence for a moment. "Are all Irish girls that stubborn?" he asked, a little crease deepening beside his mouth.

"Are all Italians so thoroughly pigheaded about getting what they want?"

They couldn't help smiling at each other. "Crista," said Phil. "Do me a favor. I'll drop the idea of the column over lunch if you'll agree to reconsider it. Tell me a little about yourself."

Pad and pencil were nowhere in evidence. But she didn't doubt for a minute that he was making mental notes. If he was half the man she thought he was, he wouldn't give up until he'd changed her mind—or something better came along. Yet to her surprise she found him amazingly easy to talk to and almost totally lacking in the arrogance she'd suspected him of. It was infinitely more comfortable to tell him about being an only child brought up by her strict and exceedingly devout grandmother than it would have been to maintain a sullen silence throughout the meal. It took enough doing simply to fend off the strong sexual energy that emanated from him and deal with the corresponding feelings it aroused.

Her keen awareness of Phil as a man had only grown by the time lunch was over. Yet Crista was in a decidedly mellow mood. In his company she felt part of the larger universe of couples, though she didn't know him well. She hadn't even complained when the waitress had brought her pastrami instead of corned beef. Pastrami was Italian, after all—like him and therefore appropriate.

"Sorry, but it's time to pop the question again," Phil remarked as he held the restaurant door open for her.

Crista shivered as they stepped out onto the sidewalk. The wind off the lake was particularly strong that afternoon and it buffeted them with a frigid blast. She could feel her eyes watering, her nose getting red.

"I'm desperate for a topic," he went on as if he didn't notice the cold. "And I think the issue of virginity versus sleeping around is a hell of a timely one. Might I ask you to reconsider? I swear on my honor as a son of Italy... no one will recognize you."

A bundled-up crowd of noontime shoppers and lunch-goers parted around them and Crista spotted a few familiar faces from the paper in its ranks. Several colleagues glanced at them with frank curiosity, and she supposed there'd be talk. Even so, she didn't want to say goodbye.

"Well," she answered hesitantly, knowing she was probably making a huge mistake, "I suppose I *could* talk to you...."

"You won't regret it!" Phil's eyes glowed with pleasure as he quickly translated "maybe" into a firm commitment. "If you could come over to my desk for a few minutes now," he said, "nobody will bother us."

"Sorry. I can't."

"But I thought..." Impulsively he caught her hands in his, willing her with all the force of his personality not to change her mind.

"I can't *right now*," Crista explained, withdrawing her hands and thrusting them into her coat pockets. "I have a hearing to cover this afternoon."

Putting him on hold gave her back a sense of control she'd been lacking ever since he'd introduced himself. Masterful, sexy, cajoling Phil Catterini would just have to cool his heels until she was available.

Chapter Two

Phil spent an extremely restless afternoon. With nothing to do until the subject of his column covered her hearing and wrote about it for the next morning's paper, he had plenty of time on his hands. Crista O'Malley was very different from the women he dated, and for some reason he didn't want to think too much about the favorable impression she'd made on him.

Lackadaisically he thumbed through the mail again, reading the latest editions of *Quill*, *Editor & Publisher* and *Chicago* from cover to cover. Next he straightened up his work area, collecting stray paper clips and washing out the offending coffee cups. He'd probably interview her at his desk, and it wouldn't do for things to appear *too* messy. True, he'd always subscribed to the theory that neatness was a sign of brain-cell deficiency. But Crista obviously suffered no lack in that department. And her desk had been immaculate, despite the fact that she'd been winding up a long-term project.

She's intelligent, surprisingly sexy and more than a little dangerous, he thought with a shake of his head, propping up his feet as it started to snow. The kind of woman who could lure a man in over his head. Still a virgin at twenty-six, she was a bright, spirited and nicely packaged temptation holding out for 2.4 kiddies and an ivy-covered bungalow in the suburbs.

A moment later, he revised his opinion again. Unless his instincts were off by a mile, Crista was the type who adored big families, whereas oversize broods were anathema to him—a long-suffering middle child in a sprawling clan now headquartered in the suburb of Melrose Park.

She called him at four-thirty to let him know she was back at her desk. She'd get together with him as soon as she'd filed her story. Phil noted with approval the cultivated, slightly husky quality of her voice on the phone.

Letting the activity of a newspaper on deadline swirl around him, he leaned back to wait. It was his favorite time of day. Magical with Christmas lights, December's early blue dusk had settled over the city. The usual traffic sounds were partially muffled by a veil of snowflakes. Yet it was a lonely hour, too, he acknowledged. People thought about rushing home to someone they cared about. He wondered if Irene would be back for the holidays and found to his surprise that he didn't much care one way or the other.

Just then his stomach rumbled, reminding him that he was hungry again. Despite a healthy appetite and the sometimes lazy ways he'd adopted now that he didn't have to cover a beat, he had the metabolism of a racehorse. It had helped him survive and stay lean in a family where three main dishes and a side of spaghetti *alla rustica* were standard fare at Sunday get-togethers.

Though his mother's cuisine was out of this world, he wasn't much of a cook himself. His roommate, the photographer who had vanished into the Central American jungles with Irene, usually did any necessary grocery shopping for the two of them. At the moment, his bachelor larder contained exactly one can of tuna, some moldy cheese and the questionable leftovers from his most recent visit to Chinatown.

Maybe I should interview Crista over dinner, he thought. I hate to eat alone.

City side, Crista was sending her story via computer to the copy desk. She had the feeling it wasn't her best effort. Nonetheless it was a relief to be finished with it. All afternoon, hanging out at the courthouse and taking notes once the hearing had gotten under way, she hadn't been able to get Phil out of her mind. His lean but powerful frame and tawny eyes had completely obliterated both Greg and Tony from her thoughts.

For God's sake don't get hung up on Phil Catterini, she warned herself in disgust as she cleared her desk. Your dilemma is just grist for his mill. He's not interested in you as a person—let alone as a potential mate.

Make that *date*, she amended hastily, chagrined at the Freudian slip as she ducked into the ladies' room to put on fresh lipstick and run a comb through her hair. Any way you sliced it, Phil wasn't husband material. According to the rumors that circulated around the *Tribune* offices like a flock of crows, he'd been engaged to half the female staffers under forty and he wasn't married yet.

"Hi... I'm ready if you are," she said, sauntering over to his desk.

To her surprise, instead of waving her to a chair he donned a rumpled tweed jacket and offered to hold her coat. "I thought we might have dinner," he suggested. "I know a place...."

The restaurant of his choice, tucked away in a North Side neighborhood not far from her apartment, had used-brick walls, red-and-white-checked tablecloths and fat wax candles in wrought-iron holders, which cast a mellow glow over everything. The chef was family, Phil informed her—his sister's husband's first cousin.

Seated across from Phil in a secluded alcove, Crista let him order for her. She wasn't disappointed in the fresh green salad and veal scaloppine smothered in a delicate sauce that hinted of Marsala and Emmenthal cheese; or in the wine he ordered.

He didn't seem in a hurry to get down to business. For her part, she'd all but forgotten her unseemly struggle with Tony the night before. As she and Phil savored their food, sipped their wine and traded shoptalk, she felt as if she were adrift on a sea of contentment. The sensation was only heightened by hidden undercurrents of excitement she couldn't ignore.

Their hands brushed as they reached simultaneously for the last chunk of crusty bread, and immediately the jolt of sensual awareness that had flowed between them earlier reasserted itself. "Let's share," she suggested casually, breaking the chunk in half and handing one piece to him.

The spell between them was broken when Phil's cousin-by-marriage brought complimentary dishes of cannoli to their table. Beaming at their compliments on the meal, he gave Crista an approving look. *"I like this girl better than the last one,"* he remarked to Phil in Italian. *"Maybe this time you get serious, huh?"*

Embarrassed, Phil shook his head. For some unknown reason, he had almost answered *yes*.

Crista demanded a translation the moment his cousin left the table. "It was nothing... an inside joke," he muttered, getting out his slim reporter's notebook. "If you don't mind, let's get started on the interview. I'm way behind schedule. As it is, I'll have to go back to the office and knock out a rough draft tonight."

Remembering the purpose of his invitation and feeling as if she'd dawdled unconscionably over the meal, Crista renounced all thought of being anything more to Phil than a last-minute source. "What do you want to know?" she asked.

As if to confirm her assessment of the situation, he assumed a professional manner. He looked alert, interested and appropriately skeptical. "Tell me about your principles and why they're important to you," he said. "The conflict they've caused you in the dating scene. What kind of men do you run into? What do they expect? Do you really consider yourself the last twenty-six-year-old virgin in Chicago? Or do other young women feel as you do?"

It was quite a barrage of questions. "I'm probably not the *only* one," she acknowledged, answering the last one first. "But I don't know anyone else who feels as strongly about this as I do. That's one of the things I'd like to find out through the column since I've decided to go ahead with it—whether your readers think I'm a throwback, an anachronism. Or if some of them agree with me. It might help if I didn't have to feel like the last of a dying breed."

Scratching across the pages of his notebook, Phil's pencil produced an illegible scrawl. "Is that how you feel?" he asked.

"Sometimes. It used to be that nice girls didn't. Now they're *expected* to, or there's something wrong with them. Most of the single women I know go to bed with their dates as a matter of course."

"Yet you don't. Why?"

"Because I don't think it's right."

Sighing, Crista took a sip of expresso and pushed her cannoli with its load of calories aside. How could she make him understand what she felt? She'd told him about the conservative background over lunch—only-child status, parochial school and strict upbringing by her Irish grandmother following her parents' death in an auto accident. But not about her sense of isolation and the longing she'd always felt to be part of a large, loving family. Would it make sense to him if she explained that her convictions weren't just something she'd picked up in catechism class? That she viewed them as an integral part of making her dream of a happy marriage come true.

"When I pledge to love a man for the rest of my life, I want to bring him something special," she said softly. "I believe sex is a privilege to be enjoyed as part of a lifetime commitment, not something to be squandered in casual affairs. And yet..."

He raised one eyebrow, inviting her to continue.

"And yet my married friends who slept around when they were part of the dating scene seem to have good relationships with their husbands. At least, so far."

"So they haven't suffered for espousing a more flexible moral code. Whereas you..."

"Whereas I think it would bother me. I'd feel that something precious had been irretrievably lost."

"Yet I'm told you're thinking of giving up...joining the crowd, so to speak. Why?"

Though she shrugged, he sensed the issue was a deeply important one to her. "Once my virginity is gone, maybe it won't matter so much," she said. "If and when Mr. Right comes along, I'll be able to hang on to him."

Neither of them said anything further for a moment.

"I'm counting on your promise not to identify me," Crista then added nervously. "I could be a laughingstock at the courthouse if anyone found out about this. And if my grandmother ever got wind of it..."

"She wouldn't understand?"

Crista rolled her eyes, evoking a grin from him. "Her moral outrage would make the saints turn over in their graves!"

"Not to worry." His brow furrowed a little as they got back down to business. "Is marriage really that important to you at twenty-six?" he asked. "You're just beginning your career. Surely there's plenty of time for a husband and family later."

I wonder how old he is, Crista thought. Thirty-four? Thirty-six? Just about the perfect age for a prospective husband. "A woman's twenties are her best childbearing years," she told him.

Though he groaned inwardly, his emotions didn't show on his face. He'd been right about her, then. "I take it you'd like a large family," he said.

"Maybe it's not responsible from an environmental standpoint. But, yes. I'm not sure I've explained myself very well...."

Ah, but you have, he thought. You're just like my mother, my married sisters and my brother's wives. Even though some of them have careers of a sort, home, hearth and a passel of screaming kiddies are where it's at for them. I'm the only male in my family over twenty-one who isn't trapped in a domestic routine.

"The problem is getting to know any man well enough to think of marrying him," Crista continued. "As you must realize, that would be true whether I was twenty-six or thirty-five. Guys these days won't wait if you're not willing to hop straight into bed. Not too long ago I lost a really special man by standing on principle. There aren't many like him around—special, I mean."

Phil's frown deepened at her words. With her domestic bent and old-fashioned outlook, Crista O'Malley was hardly his cup of tea. Yet he didn't like the thought of her mooning over some jerk who had disappointed her. "Tell me what happened," he said.

A distinct expression of sadness crept into her eyes. "He told me he respected me. And then asked someone else to marry him."

"Someone he *had* been sleeping with, I suppose?"

She nodded.

Phil's pencil paused in its journey over the narrow-lined sheets of his notebook. "I'm sorry," he said. "That must have hurt like hell."

"It did. I'd like to think I'm getting over it."

Unobtrusively a waiter brought more expresso.

"I have a feeling it was that experience which prompted you to question your values...begin to regard them as more of an albatross than an asset," he remarked when they were alone again.

"That and the wrestling match I got into last night."

What kind of bum would try to force himself on this spirited but delicate young woman? he wondered. "You said there aren't that many good men around," he reminded. "I take it the guy you were out with last night doesn't fit into that category?"

In Crista's opinion, the conversation was getting too maudlin for words. A dash of humor was sorely needed. "Actually he's harmless enough," she said. "Tell you what...I'll draw you a diagram."

Phil's interest quickened as she took out her own notebook and drew a large circle on one of the blank pages.

"That," she explained, "represents all the men in the world."

A smaller circle inside it signified "all the men in the Chicago area." Quickly she narrowed the field still further, excluding "men who are too old for me, married men, ne'er-do-wells, egomaniacs, your basic slugs or couch potatoes, assorted criminals, womanizers and general creeps."

Approaching the center, the smallest circles eliminated "all men who spend three nights a week or more with Mom and those who keep multiple cans of Cheese Whammy in their refrigerator."

"This," she said, dimpling as she stabbed the center of her diagram with a single dot, "represents the men who are left. You can see the problem."

Phil had to laugh despite himself. "I'm afraid so," he acknowledged. "But is there really such a dearth of eligible men? And what's wrong with guys who stock up on Cheese Whammy? Is that such a crime?"

"Actually, most of the men I've gone out with have been decent types," she admitted with a mischievous twinkle in her eyes. "As for Cheese Whammy...unlike *you*, guys who live on that stuff never take a woman out to dinner in a nice restaurant."

Surprised to find himself wishing the evening didn't have to end, Phil offered to drive Crista home. They shook hands politely outside her apartment building. He waited until she'd unlocked the outer door and disappeared inside with a little wave.

With deadline pressing, he returned to the office, now mostly empty except for editors and those reporters assigned to the night shift. He had the feature section all to himself.

Entering his personal code into the computer, he called up the logo and byline he'd created so many hours before. For a moment he stared at the screen, his eyes dreamy, unfocused. Then, keeping in mind the way Crista had looked when she told him about the man who got away, he began to write.

Phil wasn't at his desk the following morning when she arrived at the office. Probably he finished up the column really late last night, she guessed, and decided to sleep in. Though she was dying to learn what he'd written, she knew better than to ask. She was crazy even to stroll past the feature department. What if he *had* been here? she asked herself. He'd have thought you were having second thoughts about talking to him. Or that you had interpreted last night's dinner as something more than it really was.

So determined was she to put Phil out of her mind, she nearly jumped when Harry Jenkins mentioned noticing them leave the building together.

"You two seeing each other?" the graying, bespectacled editor asked in his blunt fashion. "If so, Phil's showing more taste than I gave him credit for."

Blushing furiously, Crista thanked him for what she decided was a compliment.

Wednesday at five in the morning, shivering in her woolly slippers and heavy robe, Crista gathered up the paper. What if he's treated the whole thing as a joke? she wondered, pouring out a mug of black coffee with trembling fingers and going to the window seat in the living room. If so, I don't think I'll be able to bear it. With her coffee cooling on the sill beside her, she began to read Phil's column.

Picture yourself in a time warp. Imagine it's the fifties again. Hamburgers and gasoline are dirt cheap. America is at the peak of her political and economic power. The family that prays together stays together. And nice girls don't fool around.

If you're a guy, you appreciate that. Sure, you try to "make out" with your girl in the back seat at the drive-in movie show. You're only human, after all, with natural human urges. But when you marry, you'll expect your bride to be a virgin. It's what society expects, too. As you stand there beside her at the altar, you're bursting with pride that she saved herself for you alone.

Now, hit the Fast Forward button and let's travel back to today. In the process, turn the expectations of the fifties inside out like yesterday's socks. Thanks to the Pill and the new permissiveness, nice girls *do* these days. In fact, they have to, one young woman told me recently—or they get left out of the matrimonial running altogether.

Though it's been something of a struggle for her, the young woman I'm talking about hasn't given in to this kind of thinking yet. Like the nice girls of the fifties, she believes marriage is the commitment of a lifetime. She regards sex as a privilege to be enjoyed within its framework. Kate, as I'll call her, is still a virgin at twenty-six. And she's paid a heavy price for her ideals.

Her eyes wide with fascination, Crista scanned the column of type, rapidly absorbing Phil's sensitive account of her tribulations with men. She had to admit he'd handled her loss of Greg to a twenty-two-year-old vamp with a deft touch. Just as she had done during dinner in the little Italian restaurant, he'd relieved the topic's seriousness with a humorous, almost flippant account of her diagram; and then reassured the reader that no, she wasn't a man-hater—not by any stretch of the imagination.

Despite the way they've treated her, Kate has good things to say about most of the men she's dated. But I get the distinct impression she's beginning to wonder if she's at fault, not them.

Not quite, Crista thought. But close.

Lately, she's been thinking of throwing in the towel. Thanks to the losses and humiliation she's suffered, she's begun to regard her virginity as an albatross, a straitjacket that's keeping her from cultivating the kind of love relationship she wants—one that might ripen into marriage and a family someday. She's begun to think about getting her initiation into sex "over with," perhaps with an accommodating stranger.

A bit shy though a very spirited young woman, Kate wasn't eager to let me interview her. It's my feeling she agreed primarily because she was curious about what you, the reader, might think.

Is Kate the last twenty-six-year-old virgin in Chicago? Or are there others like her who've been too embarrassed to speak their minds? Should she toss her principles overboard and succumb to the new morality? Or shouldn't she? Help her decide.

Hugging herself in the window seat and looking out at the gray, snowy morning, Crista felt warmth, relief and a twinge of fatalism. The warmth and relief were directed at Phil, who hadn't made fun of her. Incredibly, he'd understood. As for the fatalism, she had a sudden, irrational conviction that matters had been taken out of her hands. Maybe she *would* let the readers decide.

With an appointment scheduled that morning in nearby Berwyn, Phil stopped by his parents' house. Naturally, his father had left many hours earlier to oversee the vast, pre-dawn operation of Joseph Catterini & Sons, purveyors of fresh vegetables and fruit to Chicago's finest restaurants.

But the family home was far from deserted. As usual, the kitchen was a whirlwind of activity with his mother and Great-Aunt Rosa bustling about, the twins—now twenty—gulping breakfast before heading off to their college classes and two of his married sisters dropping off their pre-school-age children on their way to work. In a quiet corner of the family's spacious breakfast nook, Phil's maternal grandfather, Santo Marchese, smoked his pipe as he read the morning paper.

"Figlio mio!" Dusting her hands on her apron, Phil's mother gave him a welcoming hug. "It's so good to see you, my darling. Why have you stayed away so long?"

He shrugged, awkwardly patting her shoulder. "I've been busy, Mama. You know how it is."

"That's what you always say." With a smile, Luisa Catterini wiped a grandchild's runny nose and handed the boy a piece of toast. "A man should come to see his mama, though."

Unable to stop himself, Phil thought of Crista's diagram. "Not more than twice a week," he said.

She gave him a funny look.

For once, Santo didn't say hello to his favorite grandson or offer him a place at the table. "Did you read Phil's column this morning, Luisa?" he demanded instead, in his gravelly voice.

"Not yet, Papa. What with making ravioli for the church supper and getting breakfast for everyone..."

"Maybe you better, then. He took a survey this time...whether some young girl should go to bed with the men she dates. I think it's a disgrace!"

"Any letters yet?" Crista asked, stopping by Phil's desk as she was leaving the office Friday night. She hadn't heard from him since their interview and the suspense was killing her.

He looked up with a grin, letting his eyes travel down her trim but shapely figure and then return to her face. "I was just about to come over to see you," he said. "We've had quite a few. I wondered if you'd like to go over them with me. I plan to do a follow-up."

Crista smoothed the skirt of her red wool suit. "I suppose I could. What did you have in mind?"

"Are you busy Sunday morning?"

On Sundays her grandmother expected Crista to accompany her to church. But it wouldn't hurt to disappoint Gran just this once, she reasoned. After all, she had a chauffeur to drive her. "Not really," she answered.

"Well, how would you like to come over to my place? Read the papers, have breakfast? We could go over the letters then."

With a few etchings thrown in? Crista wondered, then realized she was daydreaming. In Phil Catterini's eyes, theirs was purely a business relationship. She definitely wasn't his type.

"All right," she agreed. "Mind telling me what the general run of response has been?"

"About three-to-one against your giving up the fight. My mother was fit to be tied. She insists I bring you out to the house to meet her, so she can talk you out of doing something you'll regret."

Phil's apartment faced Lincoln Park across Lake Shore Drive. Unlike the one Crista shared with Laurin Hayes a few blocks away, it was large, airy and filled with an eclectic mixture of abstract art, modern furnishings and valuable-looking antiques. It was also somewhat untidy.

He answered the door looking virile and slightly the worse for sleep in an old rugby shirt and jeans so ancient they were frayed at the knees. There was a shadow of beard on his chin and Crista found herself wanting to reach out and rub its graininess with her fingertips.

"Sorry about the mess," he murmured, showing her inside. "My roommate's away right now. We'll have the place all to ourselves."

Male or female? Crista wondered. She didn't want to ask.

Though she probably wasn't aware of it, Crista looked as cuddly as a kitten in her ivory wool slacks and matching angora sweater. Phil wanted to stroke her hair, caress the delicate ridge of her spine and cup her shapely derriere in his hands. He itched to kiss her softly parted lips.

Hands off, he told himself firmly as she took a seat. Even if Irene *has* been gone three months, this girl is a virgin, remember?

"Have some orange juice," he offered, waving at a carafe and two stemmed glasses that stood on a low table. "The coffee will be ready in a moment."

Breakfast consisted of doughnuts out of a bag. But at least they were fresh. As she and Phil scanned the newspapers at opposite ends of his contemporary overstuffed couch, Crista thought how nice it would be if the occasion were truly a social one. She felt relaxed, yet tinglingly aware of him. He's nothing like the men I usually go for, she thought. More of a diamond in the rough, for all his literary talent and intellect.

Inevitably they moved closer together when Phil got out the letters. "These are the *pro* group," he said, handing her the smaller of two stacks. "And these are against."

Crista shook her head as she leafed through some of the responses. *Go for it, baby,* a cool cat of eighteen had written. *Try it, you'll like it,* a forty-five-year-old man suggested. A preachy-sounding woman offered her opinion that sex between consenting adults was always right, whether or not they were married. *Where were you during the sexual revolution?* she asked in a sarcastic tone.

As Phil had remarked, however, most of the letters supported Crista's point of view. *Don't give in,* they chorused in unison. *I have a daughter your age,* one man of fifty had written. *I agree with your values even though she doesn't. Don't despair in your search for the man who will honor your innocence. When you find him, you'll be glad you waited. To go along with the crowd now simply because it's easier would destroy your self-respect.*

Phil's hand accidentally brushed her knee several times as they went through the letters. She pretended not to notice. But when they came across the proposal of marriage from a biochemist at a large pharmaceutical company, caution fell by the wayside.

"He says he's a virgin, too, and that he's been looking for me all his life." Crista chuckled. "Among the formaldehyde and petri dishes, I suppose. He sounds like the answer to all my prayers!"

"What's this I detect?" Phil shot back. "A double standard?" But he was laughing, too.

Just then, some of the letters slid off Crista's lap and they reached simultaneously to recapture them. Somehow their arms seemed to get entangled, their breaths to mingle. Slowly they straightened to look into each other's eyes.

"Crista..." Phil began, his hand resting on her hip.

Awash in the golden light from his tawny gaze and the wild, fluttery sensations mere contact with him seemed able to arouse, she didn't answer. A moment later, his mouth had descended on hers.

Chapter Three

Crista's first overwhelming sense was one of recognition, as if she'd been poised for a lifetime to meet his kiss. *Phil!* she thought incredulously. *I don't believe it. But* you're *the man I've been waiting for!*

It was impossible, surely. Totally incomprehensible by the light of reason or any other standard that someone who believed in shared values and well-established mutual interests might care to name. As far as Crista could tell, she and this casual, confirmed bachelor who went through fiancées—and no doubt lovers—the way most people disposed of junk mail and yesterday's newspaper, had nothing in common but their profession. They could have no earthly hope of a future together.

Yet, from the moment his lips touched hers, she *knew*, with the fierce and unshakable kind of knowing that springs from the heart. A primal resistance she'd only peripherally acknowledged gave way, allowing floodgates to open. For the first time in her twenty-six years, she longed to give without reservation.

Her soft sigh of surrender was like a goad. For Phil, it was as if someone had thrown gasoline on a bonfire, causing it to blaze up in a chimney of flame. Though he hadn't guessed it, couldn't possibly have foreseen the truth, he'd literally been starving for this petite, high-principled woman. With her tender lips and deliciously rounded breasts beneath that cloud-soft sweater, she was like ambrosia sent to him from the gods. He was powerless to resist.

With a groan, he deepened his kiss. Forcefully his tongue invaded her mouth to plumb moist, sweet depths that inflamed him even further. One of his hands tangled in her hair, which smelled faintly of green apples and had the texture of coarse silk as it spilled through his fingers. With the other, he hauled her up tightly against him, avidly learning the shape of her body. She was as pliant, as beautifully made as he'd imagined. He felt himself go taut and heavy with desire.

For her part, Crista had never known such powerful physical sensations. Wildfire raced along her veins, igniting her skin with heated chills. A deep crucible of need opened inside her—vast, empty and aching. Only he could fill it, with the very essence of himself. *I want him,* she thought in amazement—more than I knew it was possible to want a man. I'm wild to give him everything.

For Phil, union with Crista had become a white-hot desire. He burned to sweep her off her feet and carry her to his king-size bed, undress her with loving haste. Yet, as she pressed closer still, twining her arms around his neck, he hesitated. *No,* he thought, burying his face against the warmth of her neck. We can't do this. Not if I have a spark of decency left in my soul.

She caught her breath as he drew back to grasp her by the shoulders.

"Crista," he growled, his voice faintly nasal as if he'd suddenly acquired a head cold. "Forgive me. I swear I didn't have this in mind when I asked you up here today. Under the circumstances, I knew better than that."

She didn't say anything for a moment. He's rejecting me, she thought in anguish. I'm not woman enough for him. Yet a part of her knew he simply didn't want to take advantage of her. Well, I'd have stopped us if he hadn't, she told herself. *Wouldn't* I? It came as something of a shock to realize she couldn't answer that question with any certainty. Huge green eyes regarded him in consternation.

"I know you didn't plan this," she whispered at last, shaken to the core. "I... We... It was just a kiss."

But they both knew it had been much more than that. Reluctantly Phil dropped his hands. He felt like the heel of the century, some sort of depraved Casanova who had narrowly escaped deflowering an innocent.

To think you could even contemplate such a thing after winning her confidence and listening to all her private hopes and dreams, he castigated himself. You ought to be awfully damn proud.

"I take full responsibility for what happened," he said stiffly, wishing she would slap his face.

"Oh, please..." Sitting there with some of the letters scattered at her feet and the remains of their coffee and doughnuts littering the tabletop, Crista felt awkward, unsure how to handle the situation. She decided that maybe she'd better go.

Unsteadily she got to her feet.

Sensing her intention, Phil experienced a moment of panic. Though she was off-limits for a casual affair, he realized to his consternation that he couldn't let her walk out of his apartment and his life without suffering a genuine feeling of loss.

"Stay," he urged gruffly, astonishing them both. "Two adults can enjoy a Sunday afternoon... get to know each other without rekindling the Chicago fire, can't they? It's a beautiful day even if the temperature's below freezing. What would you say to a walk in the park?"

I don't want to be in love with him, Crista told herself—any more than he wants to feel that way about me. Yet, as she strolled down the winding paths of Lincoln Park with Phil at her side and one gloved hand held lightly in his, she felt extraordinarily happy and carefree. It was indeed as if fate had taken a hand.

Several times their shoulders brushed and she had the odd yet satisfying hunch that they could be friends. Not without an undercurrent of desire running through the relationship, of course. Between them, apparently, anything else was too much to expect. But with the kiss they'd shared and its aftermath, a sort of crisis had passed. They might now have a breather in which to find out more about each other.

Though it was windy and cold, the sky was a thin, clear blue with barely a trace of industrial haze. Between the stark shapes of the trees, they could glimpse the lake. Already the water close to the shore had frozen into a thin layer of ice.

She noted again that Phil didn't seem to feel the cold. Though he'd wound a scarf about his neck, his coat hung open. He was bareheaded, whistling jauntily in the chilly air. I'd like to see him on a beach, Crista thought. A real beach, not one like this—a beach with palm trees, white sand and turquoise water. I'll bet he looks fabulous in swimming trunks.

As they walked, they said very little. Yet the silence between them felt easy, unhurried, an unbelievably comfortable thing. Like them, numerous other Chicagoans had availed themselves of the bright Sunday. They passed young people, old couples out for their daily constitutional, children in bright jackets and caps, hell-bent on trudging ankle-deep through the snow.

Phil paused once to return a Frisbee to some shabbily dressed youths. Several minutes later, Crista insisted they stop for a closer look at a toddler on a sled. The toddler's parents smiled fondly, proud of their little one. The child himself was bundled to his eyelashes.

When they reached Montrose Harbor, Phil suggested they retrace their steps and return to his living room. "You look like you could use another cup of coffee, and I have a few more letters to show you," he remarked. "If you wouldn't mind going over them, I'd like to get your reaction."

"All right," Crista said.

The letters she hadn't seen yet fit into two distinct categories. The first group was from people who felt certain Phil had been putting them on. Irritably they insisted he'd made up the young woman he'd called "Kate." Girls like her simply didn't exist in today's world.

The second group, which amounted to just three responses, was from self-confessed virgins like herself. *Thank you so much for your column,* a twenty-three-year-old graduate student from Evanston had written. *Before I read it, I thought I was the only holdout around. Now I suspect there are quite a few of us out there. Please tell "Kate" not to give up the fight.*

While she pored over the letters, Phil sipped a glass of wine and closely watched her face from an easy chair, which was positioned a safe distance away. "Well?" he asked when she'd finished. "What do you think? Have they helped you make up your mind?"

How could she tell him her virginity had become a moot point where the rest of the dating scene was concerned—while remaining a critical issue between the two of them? Unexpectedly she'd found the man she wanted, the man she'd been waiting for. I only wish it didn't have to be him, she thought. We don't stand a chance.

"Getting some support for my point of view and hearing from other women who've taken the same position I have is encouraging," she said. "As for any decision-making, I'll have to think it over."

"Fair enough."

To her surprise, Phil didn't press. Instead, he proposed they turn on the television set. "The Bears are playing Green Bay this afternoon," he announced as if stating a fact of great historical significance. "Why don't you stick around if you have nothing better to do? I'll order in a pizza if we get hungry later."

As an invitation, it was first cousin to a backhanded compliment. Nonetheless, Crista felt secure enough to accept. The truth was, she wanted to stay.

"Okay," she answered, "as long as you promise not to melt Cheese Whammy over the anchovies."

I must be crazy, falling for him this way, she thought, kicking off her shoes and curling up in the corner of the couch. No good can possibly come of it. Yet despite her qualms it turned out to be the perfect afternoon—relaxed, cozy, almost serene. Crista, whose tastes ran more to symphonies and documentaries on public television, found the muted roar of the game and Phil's occasional grunts or comments a surprisingly congenial accompaniment to the Sunday book reviews, editorial page and crossword puzzle.

To nobody's surprise, the Bears won by a comfortable margin. Instead of turning off the set, Phil switched over to an old movie and they discovered they were both William Powell fans. Apparently feeling more at ease, he returned to the opposite end of the couch and put his feet up on the coffee table. When the pizza came, she ate two slices and he demolished the rest. They talked of childhood incidents and college escapades.

Outside the bank of windows that overlooked Lake Shore Drive and the park, dusk slowly gathered. Lights winked on like diamonds against velvet. At last it was time for Crista to depart.

"I really should go home, wash my hair and get ready for Monday," she said reluctantly.

Instantly Phil was on his feet. "Do you have your car?" he asked.

"No, I walked. It's only six blocks...."

"I'll drive you, then. I don't want you on the street alone after dark."

He could have called me a cab, she realized with a warm glow in the vicinity of her heart. *But he wanted to see me safely home.*

Though she'd been sure he wouldn't touch her, Phil kissed her good-night outside her apartment stoop. "When am I going to see you again?" he asked in a husky tone. "Lunch tomorrow?"

Already their lips felt familiar—totally right together. "I guess so, if you don't mind waiting until I get back from the courthouse," Crista replied.

Coming on the heels of the perfect afternoon, it was the perfect week. They shared lunch nearly every day and spent most evenings together—Christmas shopping at the Rizzoli book store in Water Tower Place, playing Scrabble with Laurin and Dan on the former's night off, even ducking into an art gallery or two as they prowled the North Michigan Avenue scene. Crista found Phil's comments about some avant-garde sculpture they viewed highly unorthodox but nonetheless filled with insight. He has a great many more facets than I initially realized, she thought.

As they got to know each other, her instinctive attraction to him only deepened. They were different in so many ways it worried her. Yet the fit seemed right. She felt surprisingly content and safe with him. Still, she wasn't sure how they'd resolve the values question. When he talked about his family, she got the distinct impression he wanted no part of marriage and children. She wondered if she'd ever be invited to meet his mama, papa, Great-Aunt Rosa, Grandpa Santo and the assorted brothers, sisters, nieces, nephews and in-laws who made up the Catterini clan. And what would her grandmother think of him?

For the time being, any hint of sex between her and Phil had been swept completely under the carpet. Though their mutual attraction continued to smolder just beneath the surface and rumors had begun to circulate around the office about their "affair," physical contact between them remained strictly limited to hand-holding and an occasional good-night kiss.

In her quieter moments, Crista thought about the question that had prompted Dan to introduce them in the first place. Thanks to that introduction the situation had changed drastically, of course. Though she hardly dared believe it yet, she'd met the man she wanted. That being the case, should she stick with her principles, come hell or high water? Or should she give way as a means of hanging on to him, allowing their relationship to ripen and grow?

Unfortunately, there weren't any easy answers. When the time comes, she tried to tell herself, I'll know what to do.

Then they attended a Friday-night Chicago Black Hawks game and the lovely, relaxed mood they'd shared seemed to vanish in a puff of smoke. Phil started out the evening in an off mood. She wouldn't have called him irascible—just distant. His air of distraction seemed only to deepen at her distaste for the game.

Never having attended a hockey game, Crista hadn't known what to expect. The spectacle struck her as violent and crude, more aggressive and brutal than any boxing match. When a free-for-all broke out on the ice with players slinging their sticks and fists in all directions, she couldn't help wincing at the injuries they sustained or the crowd's bloodthirsty yells.

"Now I know what it must have been like to watch gladiators fight in the Roman Coliseum," she remarked, wrinkling her nose in distaste as they left the amphitheater.

Phil just shrugged as if she were being too fastidious for words.

What in the world do I see in him? she wondered as they got into his late-model Japanese import. He can be so distant and sure of himself sometimes—positively detached. When it comes to emotional outlook, we're miles apart. The disparity didn't augur well if they were ever to raise children or make a home together.

You've got to be out of your mind, Catterini, old pal, Phil was berating himself. For all her sweetness and sensitivity, this girl was out of his league—a North Shore debutante brought up in a silk-padded cocoon by her wealthy grandmother. She'd never fit in with the likes of Francine, Patty and Bernadette.

The sudden realization that he'd experimentally cast her among his sisters-in-law grabbed Phil by the scruff of the neck. Hold it! he ordered himself. This is volatile stuff—a veritable nitroglycerine cocktail of the heart. Just because Crista O'Malley is a virgin and you'd like to go to bed with her doesn't mean you have to contemplate marriage. The biggest favor you could do her *and* yourself would be to drop her off posthaste at her own front door.

As luck would have it, there weren't any parking spaces on Crista's block. Keenly aware that he'd headed straight for her apartment without so much as mentioning a nightcap, she offered to run inside while he double-parked.

"No sense your leaving the car several blocks away and walking back with me just to make sure I get in safely," she reasoned in a small voice.

"Well, if you're sure you wouldn't mind..."

Their eyes met in the dark, full of unspoken thoughts. Against his better judgment, Phil leaned over to kiss her good-night.

At first, their lips barely touched, attraction and the determination not to indulge themselves in it mingling with regret. Then something deepened and yielded, like a door swinging wide to reveal a dangerous but inviting passageway. Phil's arms tightened, crushing her to him. Eagerly his mouth took possession of hers as if to satisfy the hunger of a lifetime in a single moment. I may be the worst kind of fool, he thought, reveling in the texture and scent of her, but I can't let her go.

Sighing, he leaned his forehead against hers. She could feel their blood beat in unison. "Come home with me for a while," he said, the words grainy as sandpaper on his tongue.

A thrill of anticipation overcame her, obliterating any fear. "All right," she agreed.

They didn't speak as he shoved the car into gear and drove like a maniac to his building, whipping around corners and wheeling his white compact into the underground garage with a raucous squeal of rubber on concrete. The silence between them only lengthened as they shot up to his eighth-floor apartment in the hushed, oak-paneled elevator. Crista's heart was fluttering in her throat as he unlocked the front door.

Though the foyer was pitch-dark, Phil didn't switch on a light. The faint gleam of moonlight and the city at night was visible from the living-room windows. Drawn by the subtle but powerful lures they'd tried to ignore for a week, they moved into each other's arms.

"Crista..." he confessed, gathering her to him, coat to bulky coat. "I almost decided tonight that we shouldn't see each other again...."

"I knew what you were thinking," she whispered.

"But I couldn't go through with it, sweetheart. Maybe it's a mistake, but I don't care about that. I want you too much."

Kissing her eyelids, her nose, her mouth, Phil took off her coat and removed his own. She was shapely yet petite—a trim, delicate woman with above-average looks, a cloud of dark hair and a roses-and-cream complexion. In the flat shoes she'd worn to the game, she barely reached to his chin. Suddenly he wanted to fight off the world, slay dragons for her sake. He hadn't felt that way about a woman since he'd been in love with his teacher in the third grade.

I'm desperate to ravage and protect her, he acknowledged, the discovery arousing him to greater need. In that intimate embrace, he knew it wasn't any secret that the desire to ravage was uppermost.

For Crista it was as if the earth had tilted, transforming and rearranging every precept she'd held dear. Yet she wasn't afraid, not the slightest bit hesitant. *This* is what I want, she thought, acceptance rising in her like a flood. This time and place, this man to be everything I'll ever need. I want us to blend and merge until we're irrevocably bonded to each other.

"Oh, Phil..." she breathed, her decision making itself as the last barriers tumbled.

Somehow, stumbling and holding on to each other, they made it into the living room. Gentle yet rapacious for all their finesse, his hands slipped beneath the rose-pink lamb's-wool sweater her grandmother had knitted so lovingly, and crumpled the fabric of her silk-and-lace camisole as he claimed her breasts. The sensations caused by his fingertips against her nipples were almost too exquisite to bear. Swift arrows of longing sped from her hardening buds to the core of her femininity. She wanted to give him everything.

Burdened by inexperience, she feared it wouldn't be enough. "Teach me, show me what to do," she pleaded, burning out of control as she caressed his lean, tall body. "I want so much for it to be right...."

Phil's hands stilled at her words. With a groan, he caught her against his chest. "We can't do this," he rasped, the words muffled against her hair. "I must have been crazy even to consider it."

For several seconds, Crista didn't understand. "Can't do what?" she asked in confusion, raising her face to his.

"Make love to each other." With a wrench of regret, he withdrew his hands from beneath her sweater. She was so soft, so womanly, so sensually captivating. But he knew all too well where duty lay.

"You mean... because I'm a virgin?"

"Of course, that's what I mean!" Distractedly he ran his fingers through his hair. She wasn't making this any easier.

"But if I weren't... if I'd slept with someone else... it would be all right?"

"It's not as if you weren't up-front about the situation." Phil's tone left little doubt that the answer to her question was affirmative. "C'mon," he added gently. "I'll make you a cup of hot cocoa. And then drive you home."

Crista couldn't believe her ears. At long last she'd offered herself to a man and he'd refused her because of her innocence. Far from admiring Phil for his restraint, she found herself quivering with indignation.

"I don't want any of your damn cocoa!" she flung at him abruptly, snatching up her purse and coat. "Or your gentlemanly consideration! I'm not some kind of freak!"

"Crista... For God's sake, wait a moment. I didn't mean to imply anything like that. Can't we talk about this?"

His only answer was the heavy front door of his apartment, slamming resoundingly in his face.

When Phil recovered his composure sufficiently to race after her, the elevator doors closed in his face. A quick call downstairs to the elderly doorman confirmed that Crista had indeed stalked into the lobby and tipped him to call her a cab. She refused to come to the phone.

Women! he thought in disgust, pouring himself a double Scotch and downing a healthy swallow. You're damned if you do and damned if you don't with them. Anger warred with need, causing his body to ache for some kind of release. What'll it be? he asked himself glumly. A cold shower? Or a session with a punching bag?

The phone was ringing as Crista stormed into the living room of her apartment. Gaping at her furious mood,

Laurin murmured "Hello." After listening a moment, she tried to hand Crista the receiver. "It's Phil," she announced. "That was quick."

"I don't want to talk to him!"

"He says it's urgent."

"So's my peace of mind."

From the sanctuary of her bedroom, Crista heard her roommate try to soothe Phil's ire and encourage him to try again later. When at last Laurin hung up, the phone rang again. "I won't talk to him," Crista reiterated at the top of her lungs, still steaming as she stripped off her clothes and got ready for bed.

"Not to worry... It's Dan."

Some of the wind went out of her sails at that. But she was still fuming sufficiently to feel the need for some kind of action.

During the half hour or so Laurin chatted in low tones with her steady date, Crista had ample time for thought. Gradually she came to a decision: *So he won't make love to me unless I've slept with someone... well, we'll just see about that!*

Moments after Laurin said goodbye to Dan, Crista emerged in flannel nightgown and heavy robe. There was a set look to her jaw. "What are you doing?" her roommate asked warily as she began dialing the phone.

"Calling Phil."

"I don't think he's going to like what you have to say."

The phone rang several times before Phil answered. When he did, Crista could hear the shower running in the background. She imagined him dripping wet and naked, groping for a towel.

"Crista?" he asked, a guarded hopefulness partially supplanting his irritation.

"Yes, it's me."

"I'm glad you called. Could you hang on a second while I turn off the water?"

"This won't take long."

Something about her tone warned him he'd better brace himself. A moment later, he knew his instincts had been correct.

"I'm calling you in your capacity as the writer of 'Catbird Seat,'" she continued, her tone as cold and impersonal as she could make it. "I thought you might like to know.... Kate has finally made up her mind. She's planning to get rid of her virginity once and for all—with the first clean, sober and halfway respectable stranger who presents himself."

Chapter Four

"You can't possibly be serious about this!"

The muscles tensing in his neck and forearms, Phil leaned pugnaciously over Crista's desk. It was Monday morning and they hadn't spoken to each other all weekend. Though he'd tried to contact her several times, she'd spent the past two days hiding out at her grandmother's house in Wilmette.

His tone was heated and his tawny eyes drilled into hers as he invaded her personal space. But she didn't flinch.

"Tell me you didn't mean it," he demanded, softening a little. "Say you were just angry with me. I admit I deserved it. I can take a joke as well as anyone."

"I didn't intend it as a joke!"

Goaded into answering him, she gave up temporarily on the story she was composing. "If you think I'm kidding, just hang around," she added. "On second thought, maybe you'd better not. You might cramp my style!"

"Oh, for Pete's sake! Crista..."

"Who's this Pete character, anyway?" she shot back. "Do you think he'd be my type?"

Phil uttered a heartfelt oath.

She had no way of knowing how attractive and high-spirited she looked with her green eyes flashing and two bright patches of color staining her cheeks, Phil thought.

"Look," said Phil, all too cognizant of her spunk and appeal. "It's because I care about you that I'm making an issue of this. I don't plan to leave this spot until you promise me you'll do nothing of the sort."

Miffed at the ultimatum, Crista assumed her haughtiest expression. "Nothing of *what* sort?" she retorted. "That's a non sequitur if I ever heard one. I don't know what you mean."

"Yes, you do.... Going to bed with some stranger!"

Unintentionally, Phil had raised his voice. Anyone within a radius of fifteen feet would have had to be deaf not to hear him. Several reporters who occupied nearby desks eased back from their computer screens. They gazed at him and Crista with undisguised interest. One of the female staffers stifled a smirk.

"Shh!" Crista ordered in an anguished tone. "Do you want to get the whole newsroom involved? I have a right to my privacy, and this whole thing is none of your business. I didn't grant you sovereignty over my sex life just because I agreed to an interview!"

Were women unreasonable or what? Phil wondered. "Crista," he soothed, giving himself extra points for assuming the role of peacemaker. "We may not have known each other very long, but you have to realize ours is more than a professional relationship."

At first she wasn't sure she'd heard him right. For Phil, she guessed, any kind of personal attachment was a lot to concede. However nebulous it might be, commitment didn't come easily to him. She supposed that was why they'd slipped past the boundaries of columnist and source with so little fanfare.

"I appreciate your concern," she admitted, some of her resentment giving way, "even though I feel it's misplaced. I've decided I'm operating at a disadvantage on the dating scene and I plan to remedy the situation. It's that simple. Now, if you don't mind, I'd like to get back to work."

Naturally she hadn't told him the full truth. She was afraid it would send him running for the hills—permanently. And that was the very last thing she wanted.

To her chagrin, he folded his arms over his chest and arranged his legs in a position of parade rest. "Suit yourself," he answered complacently. "Until I have your word, I'm not going anywhere."

Great, Crista thought. I've got my very own six-foot-tall, hazel-eyed watchdog. With somebody like him around, who needs a chastity belt? About to let her temper flare out of control, she realized it would only make matters worse. If she lashed out at him, he'd simply create another scene.

"What if I agreed to take a break and talk this over with you in private?" she asked. "Afterward, would you promise to leave me alone?"

With a frown he considered her proposal. "That sounds fair," he conceded. "I'll get my coat."

Outside, it was bitterly cold and windy as only a city on the shores of one of the Great Lakes could be in the wintertime. With their collars turned up around their ears and their shoulders buffeted by the icy blast, they headed south, crossing the Chicago River via the Michigan Avenue bridge. Like the exhaust from a heavy concentration of cars, trucks and buses, their breath smoked and hung in the frigid air.

"What about all the reasons you gave me for preserving your virginity?" Phil asked, ducking a little so his voice wouldn't carry. "Do those just get shoved out the window?"

A shadow of vulnerability crept into Crista's eyes. "I don't want them to."

"Why must they, then?"

She turned to face him outside a well-known furrier's display window. Something made her decide to stick her neck out, if only a little way.

"If you really cared about someone and adhering to your principles was a guaranteed way of losing that person," she asked, "what would you do?"

She's still hurting over the guy who got away, he concluded, his ego absorbing the blow. What's-his-name, the attorney. I wish to hell she could get him out of her head.

"That's not a fair question," he told her.

"I don't see why."

"It's different for a guy. You know that."

"And a hearty oink-oink to you!"

Phil grinned engagingly, acknowledging she had scored. When he looked at her that way, she couldn't help warming to him. Fortunately, he hadn't guessed the full extent of how she felt.

By now, Crista believed she'd drawn a pretty accurate bead on their situation. Phil was being a gentleman in her case, but it was a lot more complicated than that. He didn't want to be the first to make love to her because he felt it would leave him obligated. In order to live with himself, he'd have to marry her. And marriage was something he definitely could do without.

I didn't ask to fall in love with you, she thought, regarding him with a mixture of exasperation and affection. It wasn't anything I could control.

Since she had, the only way she could see out of their dilemma was to shed her virginity. Once it was no longer an issue, he'd have no excuse not to make love to her. It was what they both wanted, with every ounce of passion in their souls.

We certainly can't go on as we have, wanting each other and not doing anything about it, she rationalized. We'll either become lovers or drift apart. If it was the former, she believed, Phil would eventually change his mind. He'd *want* them to have a future together.

It didn't occur to her that if she carried out her threat and had sex with a stranger, she might drive a lasting wedge between them.

Meanwhile Phil was thinking his own thoughts. Though he had a deep emotional prohibition against taking Crista to bed, he couldn't bear the idea of another man touching her. He knew firsthand what casual sex was like, and he didn't want her besmirched by it. She was too fresh, too idealistic to suffer such a fate.

Realizing she was serious about her ridiculous plan and that no argument he could advance was likely to dissuade her, he cast about for another approach. Suddenly he thought of his mother and her insistence he bring "Kate" out to the house to meet her. That's what I'll do, he determined. I'll introduce her to Mama and *she*'ll set Crista straight.

In fact, it wouldn't hurt to have Crista meet the whole family, he decided. Though the assembled members of the Catterini clan sometimes got on his nerves, Phil had to admit they were a living and breathing bastion of traditional values.

It occurred to him suddenly that Christmas was just six days away. He and Crista hadn't made any plans together. He hadn't even bought her a present. Not stopping to consider the fact that he'd taken spending the holiday with her for granted, he mulled over a plan.

"Let's have a truce," he suggested abruptly, catching her mittened hands in his. "We'll both think things over for a week. In the meantime, come for Christmas dinner with my folks."

The invitation came as a total surprise. From the first time Phil had asked her out without linking the occasion to information-gathering for his column, she'd been wondering if they'd spend any part of the holiday together. But since they'd butted heads on Friday, she'd given up hope.

Curious about his parents and his sudden eagerness to introduce her to them, she decided to accept. "All right," she told him. "I agree to your terms. I'd love to come to your parents' house for Christmas dinner...provided my grandmother's invited, too."

"Your grandmother?" Phil gave her a blank look.

"I've told you about her. If I didn't spend Christmas with Gran, she wouldn't have anyone. Besides, I *want* to be with her."

Though he was uneasy about the wealthy dowager he'd never met, Phil could hardly refuse. He only hoped any airs the old lady might project wouldn't be all that noticeable amid the hubbub of a Catterini-style celebration.

"Our big family get-together is always scheduled for Christmas night," he explained. "If it's all right with your grandmother, I'll pick up the two of you at her place around four o'clock."

Continuing to hold her hand as they walked back toward the office, Phil felt he'd won a victory of sorts. He had a lot of confidence in his mother. Unfortunately, if she succeeded, he and Crista would be back to square one, spending all their time together and struggling to stay out of bed.

* * *

Snow fell on Christmas morning, blanketing the gritty streets and outlining the trees' bare branches with a graceful tracery of white. Cozy in a flowered robe beside the Dutch-tiled hearth of her grandmother's parlor, Crista was opening gifts. The house had been chilly when they'd arisen; she and Gran had pulled their blue velvet wing chairs close to the cheerful blaze.

For Gran, Crista had chosen a turquoise quilted bed jacket, a five-pound box of chocolates—heavy on the "Trinidads"—and the latest hardcover mystery novel by Dick Francis, her grandmother's favorite author. If there was anything Mary Rose Burke loved, it was eating bonbons and reading spine-chilling mysteries in bed.

Now it was Crista's turn. She gave a little exclamation of pleasure as she removed the silver-and-blue Christmas paper from a medium-size box to reveal a pale yellow angora sweater knitted by her grandmother's loving hands.

"Oh, Gran, it's lovely!" she exclaimed. "You do such beautiful work."

Mary Rose's soft cheeks glowed pink at the compliment. She gave her granddaughter an affectionate look. "I'm glad you like it, dear child," she said. "Hurry and open the other one. I've saved the best for last."

The tiny package decorated with a sprig of holly contained a delicate string of creamy, perfectly matched pearls. Crista's eyes widened as she drew it forth.

"Isn't this the necklace you wore at your wedding?" she asked. "And my mother at hers?"

"The very same."

"I love it. But why are you giving it to me now? I'm not getting married. I'm not even engaged."

"I know." Mary Rose rested one blue-veined hand on her granddaughter's arm. "I've been watching you, darling. This time it's love, isn't it?"

"Yes," Crista admitted. "I want to spend the rest of my life with him."

Her grandmother nodded. "Then you'd best be prepared. Oh, I know... Things haven't been going smoothly for you with your young man. They rarely do at first. I remember how your grandfather..."

A fond smile playing about her mouth, Mary Rose was off and running with yet another tale of how Black Jack Burke, a handsome, devil-may-care Irishman direct from the old sod, had chased her until *she* caught *him*.

Crista listened with one ear as she held the pearls in her hand. Courtship is different now, she thought regretfully. Today's lovers must play by different rules.

Following a late brunch and a game of Scrabble with her grandmother, Crista dressed carefully for dinner with Phil's parents in a dark blue velvet frock with a softly draped skirt and white lace collar. Brushing her dark, mahogany-lit page boy until it shone, she fastened on Mary Rose's pearls. I wonder what they'll think of me? she asked herself nervously. I want to make a good impression.

She was looking out the bay window in the parlor when Phil came up the front walk. For once, he wore a full-length topcoat—though his head was bare. His cheeks were pink with cold. She could see that he was impressed by the house's sweeping porches, turrets and gingerbread trim.

Fighting a sudden case of the jitters, she ran to answer the bell. His lips were chilled but his breath warm and steamy as he bent to kiss her mouth. "Merry Christmas," he said, glancing around as if he suddenly realized her grandmother might be watching them. "You look wonderful. I brought you something."

"I have something for you, too," Crista replied. "Let's go into the parlor. Gran will be ready in just a moment."

They sat side by side on the rosewood-trimmed Victorian sofa facing the front hall and gracefully curving stairway. Crista's fingers trembled slightly as she unwrapped a new crossword dictionary from Kroch's.

"Thanks," she told him, kissing him lightly on the cheek. "This is great. I've been wanting one."

From her, Phil received a Chicago Black Hawks coffee mug. You'll have to keep this one clean, he thought ruefully as he expressed his gratitude. Turn over a new leaf.

Once their gifts had been exchanged, he and Crista couldn't seem to find anything to say to each other. For several awkward minutes the only sound in the parlor was the loud ticking of an antique clock. Phil guessed she was as apprehensive about meeting his parents as he was about being given the once-over by her grandmother.

At last, Mary Rose Burke appeared in a dark print dress with her snow-white hair arranged in an Edwardian pouf. She impressed Phil as being fragile and erect, with a sharp eye for miscreants. As Crista made the introductions, he was uncomfortably aware that she was probably looking him over as a prospective suitor for her granddaughter.

Crista's in safe hands as far as I'm concerned, he assured her silently. I'm the last guy in the world who would hit on her. The twinkle in Mary Rose's eyes made him wonder if she could read his mind.

"It's a pleasure to meet you, Mrs. Burke," he said.

If anything, the benevolent twinkle increased. "I'm happy to meet you, too, Philip," she replied. "I must admit I've been looking forward to this afternoon."

At the Catterini household in Melrose Park, Joe Catterini, Jr., answered the door and took their coats. As usual, the place was bursting at the seams. The twenty or so youngsters belonging to three of Phil's married brothers and two of his married sisters all seemed to be exuberantly underfoot.

The comfortable living room with its blaring television set was awash in Christmas paper, pull toys, talking-wetting baby dolls and rocket games. Ornaments on the huge Christmas tree teetered crazily as a little girl chased the family cat beneath its branches. A boy of about eight was noisily picking out chopsticks on the upright piano. The good-natured warnings of parents mingled with football commentary and the deep rumble of Phil's father's and grandfather's voices as they watched the game.

For Crista, it was all a bit too much. She stood tongue-tied between Phil and her grandmother as he set about the impossible task of making introductions. Meanwhile he was casting about frantically for a place to park Mrs. Burke where she wouldn't have a heart attack.

As always, it was Mama Catterini to the rescue. Quickly sizing up the situation, she bustled in from the kitchen to offer Mary Rose her hand and greet Crista with a warm hug.

"I'm so glad to meet you, and especially glad you could join us today!" she exclaimed. "As you can see, it's the more the merrier around here. Right now, the turkey's almost ready to come out of the oven. Why don't you both come with me? My father's sister Rosa will enjoy your company, Mrs. Burke. And Crista... you can help Phil's sister Angela set the table."

His family closed around them like a warm blob of acceptance and goodwill. Left behind with the men and children in the living room, Phil watched and listened with amazement as Rosa Marchese and Mary Rose Burke hit it off over the arrangement of the relish tray. Despite her shyness and the initial shock meeting his family was sure to have caused, Crista seemed surprisingly at home chattering with Angie as they set out the seemingly endless place settings of china and silverware such a large family required.

He was aware that his parents, brothers and sisters were sizing her up, comparing her with the very different sort of young women he'd brought home in the past. Probably they think I'm serious this time, he admitted. Well, they couldn't be more wrong. Yet he felt a sense of pride in Crista's fresh looks and modest behavior. He doubted if his mother had guessed her identity as "Kate." He planned to tell her as soon as he could.

A short time later, Luisa Catterini called her brood to the table. Dinner began with a prayer, followed by several rounds of toasts. Even the children, most of whom were crowded around a second table for lack of space, joined in with mugs of apple juice.

Crista quickly realized that the turkey Luisa had mentioned earlier was only the centerpiece of a huge feast. Bedlam broke out all over again as the various dishes were passed and the plates filled.

"It's a joke we always play on newcomers," Phil's sister-in-law Patty confided as she handed Crista a platter of clove-studded ham. "We keep them passing all this mouthwatering stuff back and forth until they're sure they'll never get a bite to eat!"

During the meal, Crista gradually got the family members straight in her head. At thirty-eight, Joe, Jr., was the oldest, the father of seven children. Next came Tony, thirty-seven. He and the former Francine Pulaski had four boys. Both brothers worked for their father in the family produce business as did Angie, thirty-six and the mother of five. Angie was married to Greg, a CPA.

Two years younger than Phil, Maria was thirty-two. Her husband Tom was a cop, one of "Chicago's finest." They had three children. Paolo, thirty, and his wife, Traci, had been married a year and a half. They were the parents of a six-month-old baby. Paolo, too, worked in the family business.

Margie, who was Crista's age and the wife of Dave, who drove a truck for Catterini Produce, was heavily pregnant. Twenty-four-year-old Frank, an Air-Force sergeant married to Bernadette, was a newlywed. At twenty, twins Mike and Steve were the senior Catterinis's youngest offspring. Both were going steady with girls they'd met in high school.

As a close-knit, loving family, the Catterinis surpassed Crista's wildest dreams. No wonder Phil's so secure, so special—with all that love to back him up, she thought. I wonder if he realizes how lucky he is.

At last even the crumbs of Rosa Marchese's delicious pumpkin and mince pies had disappeared. Lighting his pipe, Grandpa Santo gathered the children for a traditional round of Christmas stories. A brigade of adult volunteers was organized to do the dishes while Luisa, Aunt Rosa and Patty, who had cooperated to cook the feast, rested on their laurels.

Catching her grandmother's eye as Phil tucked a dish towel around his waist and grabbed another to join in, Crista noted a gleam of approval. I want so much for them to like each other, she thought. What the Catterinis have in such abundance, Gran and I have needed for a long, long time.

When Phil finally got a private word with his mother, it was almost time to go. He caught up with her in the laundry room, where she was stuffing two oversize tablecloths and a huge pile of napkins into the washing machine.

"One of us could've done that, Mama," he reproached.

Calmly Luisa measured out the soap. "I don't mind," she answered with a smile. "It's easier to get out the stains if you treat them right away."

Closing the washer lid, she started the cycle. "I really like your Crista," she added, turning to him. "Why didn't you tell me she was 'Kate'?"

Phil stared at her in astonishment. "How did you guess?"

"How do mothers ever find out anything?" Luisa shrugged. "Instinct, I suppose. I've been curious ever since your second column appeared. Did she ever make up her mind?"

Briefly, Phil was at a loss for words. He hadn't realized how awkward it might be to try explaining Crista's decision without alluding to the role he himself had played in it. Or destroying his mother's good opinion of a young woman he'd begun to care about.

"She told me last week she was going to go ahead," he admitted, slightly embarrassed to be discussing such a topic in the first place. "Get rid of her virginity, so to speak, with some stranger. She seems to feel that if she doesn't, she'll never get to first base with the right man when he comes along."

This time, Luisa didn't say anything. She regarded Phil with a thoughtful expression.

"I talked her into holding off for a while," he added. "I was hoping that you..."

Slowly his mother shook her head. "I'm sorry, son," she said. "I've changed my mind. I don't believe it would be a good idea for me to talk to Crista about this. But I have every confidence you'll help her to find the right solution. She's a lovely girl and I like her grandmother, too. They're both welcome in this house any time."

Phil was exceptionally quiet as he drove Crista and her grandmother back to Wilmette. I know what Mama wants, he thought. Papa, too. But they don't need another daughter-in-law, more grandchildren. I'm not cut out for married life. Still, with nothing resolved between him and Crista, he was apprehensive about what would happen next.

When they reached Mary Rose Burke's house, Crista asked if he'd mind waiting while she ran upstairs and got her things. "I have to work tomorrow and I took the train up here," she explained. "I could use a ride home if you're going in my direction."

She returned a few minutes later with her gifts and overnight bag. Loading them into his car, Phil realized they hadn't been alone together since their aborted lovemaking in his apartment. I'd like to spend time with her, he thought as they drove to her place. Find out if she's changed her mind. But he didn't want to be trapped in another wrestling match. The last one had resulted in a lose-lose situation.

As they parked near her door, Crista mentioned that Laurin and Dan were likely to be home and invited him up for a drink.

"Sure, why not?" he responded. There was safety in numbers. With her roommate and Dan around, the situation wouldn't get out of control.

To his dismay, a note was taped to the television set when they walked into the living room. "Lucked into free ballet tickets," Laurin had scrawled in an obvious hurry. "Back sometime after midnight."

Settling himself in a corner of the couch, Phil glanced around uneasily while Crista poured out tiny glasses of brandy. The place was cozy, feminine and neat. *I shouldn't be here*, he thought, his early-warning system setting off alarms. But a stubborn, willful part of him refused to go.

Crista looked very demure in her lace-collared dress as she took a seat beside him. "Here's to a wonderful Christmas," she said, clinking her glass against his. "I want to thank you again for having me and Gran over to your parents' house. You can't possibly guess what it meant to us."

Maybe I really can't, he acknowledged to himself. *Maybe Crista wants what I've always taken for granted and frequently tried to escape.* "It was my pleasure," he answered warily.

Self-consciously they sipped at their drinks as another silence lengthened between them. *Laurin and Dan won't be back for several hours*, Crista thought. *This opportunity is just too good to pass up.*

"Phil," she said, taking the plunge, "I'd like to ask you a very big favor. I've decided to go ahead with the plan we discussed last week. But I don't want to make love to a stranger. I'd like *you* to be the man who helps me carry it out."

Phil blinked in astonishment, the shock of her request lurching through his system. "No way in hell am I gonna do that!" he exploded.

"Please," she begged. "Hear me out and then refuse if you must. I trust you, Phil. And care about you. With you I wouldn't have anything to fear. I promise that aside from birth control, there'd be absolutely no obligation on your part."

Before he could get to his feet, she had twined her arms around his neck. On his, her lips were tender, inviting and lightly flavored with the liqueur they'd just drunk. Her gently rounded breasts pressed against his chest through the soft barrier of their clothing. Cursing himself for being a degenerate and a fool, he savored the remembered taste of her. Every night for the past week he had ravaged her in his dreams.

His idiot pretense that they could limit themselves to hugs and kisses collapsed when she wriggled out of her dress. Just the sight of her in her thin, lacy slip sent a hot shaft of need shivering to his groin.

"No way are you going to talk me into being part of some crazy stunt," he assured her roughly, putting a safe distance between them. "Get back into your dress or I'm outta here!"

Stubbornly Crista shook her head. "Turning me down won't change anything," she vowed. "My mind's made up."

"So is mine."

Fiercely Phil thrust his arms into his coat.

She was curled up on the couch in her robe, sipping her third B&B when Dan and Laurin returned.

"What did you expect?" Laurin asked when Crista poured out the whole sorry tale after Dan's departure. "Forcing a guy's hand never works. Surely you don't plan to go through with this harebrained scheme."

For a moment Crista quietly considered her options. "Not only do I plan to go through with it," she said, "I know just what I'm going to do. I've got several weeks of vacation time coming and I'll use one of them to get out of town. Phil won't even know what's going on."

Frowning, Laurin warned that the course of action she was contemplating could be very dangerous. "Sex with strangers can be risky these days," she reminded her.

Still smarting from Phil's refusal, Crista felt her independence flare. "Maybe so," she admitted. "But I'll be extremely careful."

Laurin fell silent.

"As for my destination," Crista added, "I have the perfect place in mind. I'm always sick of winter, once Christmas is past. And anyway, what more appropriate place could there be to lose your virginity than the Virgin Islands?"

Chapter Five

With a whirlwind burst of energy that was born of anger and frustration, Crista spent the next few days arranging for time off, making her hotel reservations and buying a round-trip ticket to Christiansted, St. Croix. There were some fantastic bargains available, thanks to rebuilding after the devastation of Hurricane Hugo and innkeepers' efforts to lure tourists back to the island.

Usually quite conservative when it came to spending money, she also blew a healthy chunk of her savings on a glamorous and unabashedly sexy wardrobe. I wouldn't dream of wearing such a minimal bikini in Chicago, she admitted, surveying her loot.

She also went to a chic department store for a cosmetics makeover. With the counter girl's help, she learned to make up her eyes so they appeared larger and more mysterious. She also adopted a brighter shade of lipstick. As long as I'm going on the prowl, she rationalized, I may as well look my best.

* * *

At the office, Crista snubbed Phil as vigorously as if he had the plague. Her fury would have known no bounds if she'd guessed Laurin had told Dan everything. She wouldn't have needed an oracle to advise her that Dan would rat to his best pal—complete with dates, destination and flight numbers. Men tended to stick together.

"Well, that's it, old buddy," Dan said to Phil over a couple of cold ones at a nearby pub. "The only thing I can't remember is the name of her hotel. What are you going to do?"

Staring at him across the scarred tabletop of their booth, Phil felt both guilt-ridden and horrified. His conscience whispered that he wasn't blameless in the affair.

Desperately he tried to think. Pleading with Crista wouldn't work, he guessed. If her purchase of a plane ticket was any indication, she was done talking on the subject. She wasn't speaking to him anyway.

"What are you going to do?" Dan repeated.

Shaking his head in frustration, Phil took a swig of his beer. "Follow her, I guess," he muttered helplessly, realizing he couldn't just sit back and let matters take their course. "That is," he amended, "if I can get Gail Hornsby to give me the time off."

Gail was his boss, the feature editor.

"You mean...traipse after Crista to the Caribbean? Act as her bodyguard?"

Grimly Phil nodded.

"Wow!" Dan whistled. "It really must be love. What if Gail refuses?"

Did he *love* Crista? Phil asked himself. He didn't know the answer. At the moment, he was too confused and upset to sort things out.

"If Gail says no," he answered, irritated with Crista for putting him in such an untenable position, "my hands are tied. She'll just have to go to perdition on her own."

Thoughtfully Dan scraped the salt off a pretzel. "I don't suppose you plan to tell her you'll be along for the ride?" he asked.

Phil gave him a disbelieving look. "Hell, no! Are you crazy? She'd have me thrown off the plane for harassing her."

By the time she was scheduled to leave for St. Croix, Crista was having second thoughts. But she didn't want to admit them to anyone. If I don't go through with my plan, she reasoned, nothing will change. Phil and I will continue at loggerheads. Ultimately I'll lose him to a girl some other guy has taken to bed.

Sleet was rattling against the windshield and coating the expressway with a dangerous film of ice as Laurin drove her to the airport.

"Be careful," Crista's friend emphasized, letting her out in front of the Pan Am sign. "Don't take any wooden nickels or flirt with any ne'er-do-wells. In other words don't do anything I wouldn't do. Umm... Better make that anything I *shouldn't* do. I wish you would change your mind."

Crista only shook her head. Checking her bags through to Christiansted, then passing her carry-on luggage through one of the airport's electronic screening devices, she started down the long, crowded corridor to her assigned gate. Outside the huge plate-glass windows, the nasty weather had only intensified. She felt terribly alone.

Maybe I should have talked it over with Phil one last time, she speculated as she showed her ticket to the gate agent and took a seat. We might have been able to come to an understanding. But she couldn't imagine what sort of understanding, or on what terms. It was too late now to change her mind.

A tall, nondescript man in a slouchy hat, dark glasses and a rumpled raincoat was seated across the room from her beside an anxious mother with two small children and a screaming baby. Absorbed in her own thoughts, Crista didn't pay much attention to him. She merely noted that his manners left something to be desired. Didn't he know better than to wear a hat indoors?

Covertly watching Crista as he fought the urge to scratch the false mustache Dan had helped him affix to his upper lip, Phil wished they were taking the trip together. *We could be having a wonderful time if I'd made love to her the way she wanted,* he acknowledged. *But thanks to his column and the way she'd shared her innermost thoughts with him, he felt oddly protective of her. Man-woman relationships sure could get complicated.*

He glanced toward the check-in counter just as the gate agent posted a twenty-minute delay. *Marvelous!* he thought. *Every minute we have to wait is another minute Crista could discover me.*

The gate area was filled to overflowing with impatient Miami-bound passengers. In his mother's arms, the baby wailed lustily. One of his siblings whined that she had to go to the bathroom.

"I hate to impose," the baby's pale, distraught mother said to Phil in a frazzled voice. "But she'll wet her pants if I don't take her. Would you mind?"

A moment later, Phil found to his astonishment that he was holding the screaming child. "Lift him up against your shoulder and pat him on the back," advised a skinny teenager who looked as if she might have baby-sitting experience. "He probably has to burp."

The baby promptly threw up on Phil's raincoat. Wrinkling his nose in disgust, he juggled the infant as he dabbed at the mess with his handkerchief. No way am I ever going to get married and father a kid like this, he decided.

Fortunately for him, when they finally called the passengers for boarding, he was seated some distance from Crista and the squalling child. Burying his nose in a magazine, he tried to imagine what life had been like before he'd gotten involved with a green-eyed spitfire who could make the blood sing in his veins. Thanks to her, his erstwhile freedom and former casual attitude toward sex had vanished overnight. Without half trying, she's turned my world upside down, he realized.

Crista was imagining Phil hard at work on his column as she stared out at a sea of dirty gray clouds from her window seat. Will he miss me? she wondered. Or simply find someone more experienced? Why, oh, why didn't I try harder to work things out with him? Memories of his angry refusal to make love to her stiffened her resolve.

Miami International was a crush of jostling bodies, a multidecibel din of Spanish and English, with a few other languages thrown in. The Pan Am gate marked Flight 178, St. Croix was smaller than the one where they'd waited at O'Hare. But it was equally crowded. Phil hovered on the fringes, hoping to avoid discovery. His seat number was called for boarding before Crista's but luckily he was stowing his carry-on bag in the overhead compartment with his face turned away from her when she brushed past.

If she'd recognized him, she'd have probably made a scene, he thought as he buckled his safety belt—maybe even complained to the stewardess. I must have been insane to follow her like this, after refusing to meet Irene for a weekend in Mexico City. I don't even care much for tropical climates.

* * *

They arrived at their destination after dark. Unlike the huge Chicago and Miami air-traffic hubs they'd passed through, the St. Croix airport was old-fashioned and built on a human scale. The plane stopped a short distance from the terminal building. No motorized, accordian-pleated jetway appeared to serve as an exit. Instead, two uniformed attendants rolled out a set of portable metal steps.

In the baggage-claim area there were hand-printed welcome signs and a single luggage carousel. Inevitably, when Phil stepped forward to retrieve the larger of his two duffel bags, Crista spotted him.

"You!" she cried in disbelief, causing the other passengers to turn around and stare at them. "What are you doing here?"

"Taking a much-deserved vacation," he answered defensively, aware that the lone airport security guard had taken a definite interest in their exchange. "It's a free country, you know. This is part of the United States."

Briefly she stared at him, chagrin and uncertainty warring in her eyes. The chagrin won out.

"Don't expect to follow me around," she snapped. "By the way, that fake mustache you're wearing is migrating toward your left cheek."

Collecting her bags, she turned on her heel and signaled to the driver from an island transportation company. Thank heaven she'd arranged in advance for her transfer to the hotel, or she and Phil might have gotten stuck sharing a taxi. At that moment, she would have preferred a chimpanzee as her companion.

As soon as she and her luggage were safely stowed in the company's blue and white van, Phil tried to hitch a ride with its driver. If he didn't stick close to her, he'd never find out where she was staying.

Shaking his head, the cheerful man told Phil regretfully that all his seats were taken. "Where you going, mon?" he asked.

"I don't know," Phil confessed. "I don't have a reservation anywhere. I just want to follow that girl in the yellow dress."

The driver grinned. "Love make a mon do strange things," he sympathized. "On St. Croix in January, you be plenty lucky to find a bed."

For Crista, the ride to Grapetree Bay and the Crescent Beach Resort was harrowing enough. The excitement began with the driver's announcement that "Here in the Virgin Islands, we drive on the left."

Before she could adjust to such a radical idea, they were off, taking corners and hilly roads at a breakneck pace. Thrown against another passenger, she clutched for a handhold. Except for the vast fairyland of lights someone said was the Amerada-Hess oil refinery, and an occasional cluster of corrugated metal shacks, it was too dark to see anything.

In the older-model, unmetered cab Phil had hired to follow her, he was experiencing a rough ride. The taxi's shock absorbers had given up the ghost long ago. Even its upholstery had seen better days. He cringed every time they turned a corner on the left, certain they'd crash headlong into someone. The lights of oncoming cars gave him a bad case of vertigo.

He was overcome by a feeling of powerlessness. To begin with, he didn't have the faintest idea where he was headed or any notion of how the island was laid out. And once he arrived at his destination, he probably wouldn't have a place to sleep.

His cab trailing Crista's van, they entered the city of Christiansted. Shuttered, somewhat shabby structures that had clearly known several centuries of use huddled together on either side of the street.

"These are some *seriously* old buildings," a tourist from Louisiana drawled.

Noting his wife's dead silence, Crista could tell she didn't care much for the looks of things.

By contrast, the area around the harbor was well maintained, elegant and quaint. Very little trace of Hugo's visit was evident. They made several stops to let off passengers in narrow, cobbled alleys and Crista caught strains of reggae music, the mellow *plonk-plonk* of steel drums. An aroma of cooking charcoal permeated the air. Shop windows glittered with a dazzling array of free-port merchandise.

She caught a glimpse of yellow government buildings and the old Danish fort before they careened out of town again, snaking over hilltop country roads with the sea in the distance. Where *is* this place I'm staying? she wondered. At the ends of the earth?

It was at that point she became aware of car lights in the van's oversize rearview mirror. "I think somebody's following us," she remarked.

The driver grinned at her. "Yes, *ma'am*," he replied.

Phil? she wondered, incredulous. Does he really expect to dog my footsteps this way?

If only he hadn't decided to follow her. She didn't want their estrangement to become permanent, and she was suddenly afraid that was just what would happen if he monitored her activities too closely. Only sheer stubbornness kept her from giving in.

For several miles the road ran along the edge of a sheer, winding cliff and Crista could see the reef, creaming with breakers just a short distance from the shore. Then their route dipped to pass several houses and what looked like a condominium development. Crescent Beach Resort came into view on her right. It was situated directly on the beach, among graceful coconut palms.

The hotel reception area was open and breeze-swept, with rattan furniture and an informal check-in desk. Dressed in sarongs or batik shirts with white cotton trousers, staff members were serving a "get-acquainted" punch that tasted as if it contained passion fruit.

Crista glared at Phil as he paid off his cabdriver and approached the desk. She could see that he had removed the offending mustache altogether. Her face took on a look of grim satisfaction when she heard someone tell him all the rooms were spoken for. Refusing to take pity on him, she turned away as he tried unsuccessfully to bribe the night manager. She'd already left for her room when he upped the ante to a twenty-dollar tip.

"It's like I tell you, mon," the night manager said in his musical English, pocketing the bill. "All the hotel rooms are full. But maybe I can let you use one of the new timeshare apartments across the road if we don't advertise the fact."

"That'd be fine," Phil answered. He peeled off another twenty, anxious to be relieved of his refugee status.

Though the man frowned, he took that bill, too. "It's not furnished yet," he warned, handing over a key he kept in his back pocket. "But there is electricity and water whenever the pump is working. I'll ask one of my people to bring over a mattress."

Entering her room, Crista tipped the bellboy and then stepped out onto her balcony. Silky palm fronds rustled a few feet from where she was standing. A full moon glimmered on gentle surf, making her wish things were different. The musical hiss and tug of larger breakers whispered to her from the reef, making her think of romance.

I'm really here, she told herself. I wonder what Phil's going to do, where he's going to sleep.

Without stopping to unpack, she removed a white linen dress with a narrow, slit skirt and matching high-heeled sandals from her garment bag. Part of her wanted to return to the lobby to see how Phil was making out. But to actually go back downstairs would be admitting defeat. Better not, she decided.

Besides, sweet old Mrs. Vandervelt from the plane had suggested they meet in the bar for a drink, and Crista didn't want to let her down. The elderly, soft-spoken woman had mentioned something about introducing her to her grandson, who lived on the island.

Depositing his bags in the empty time-share condo, which smelled of new carpet and fresh paint, Phil washed his face. Combing his hair, he changed into a T-shirt and shorts. Until his mattress arrived, there was no place to sit or stretch out in the tiny apartment except the floor. Anyway, by Chicago standards it was still early. The washboard beat of indifferently played calypso music beckoned from the resort's pool area.

If I know Crista, he thought, she won't waste any time going after her objective. He decided to walk back across the road and check out the action. He fully expected to find her ensconced on a barstool, drinking a banana banshee and flirting with someone.

To his surprise, she was seated at one of the tables with an elderly woman and a blond, deeply tanned man about her own age. Pointedly ignoring him, she appeared to chat with her two companions as if they were old friends.

For the first time that day, it dawned on Phil that there was something different about her. Unlike the clothes she wore to the office, her white linen sheath was cut to reveal the curve of her bosom and a striking length of thigh.

She'd also applied more makeup than usual. Her eyes flashed green as emeralds beneath thick, dark lashes as she crossed her shapely legs. Keeping her profile turned toward Phil as if to taunt him, she gave the blond man and his elderly companion a brilliant smile.

"Do you know who that is?" Phil asked the sarong-clad waitress who stopped by to take his drink order.

"You mean that handsome guy in the dinner jacket?" the pretty girl asked.

Annoyed, he nodded.

"That be Peter Vandervelt, from West Indian Laboratory of Fairleigh Dickinson University," she said. "Many times his grandmother stays here while she visits him."

On closer inspection, Phil recognized the elderly woman as Crista's seatmate from the plane. Damn, he thought. Of all the rotten luck. Most women on the make for the first time would turn up a gigolo or a scoundrel. Not Crista. *Her* first attempt, she bags a decent guy complete with family references!

Looking into Peter Vandervelt's friendly blue eyes, Crista tried not to think of Phil's hazel ones. Mamie Vandervelt's grandson was a very nice man, not to mention extremely good-looking. She didn't think she could go wrong choosing him.

"So you work in marine science," she remarked, using her skills as an interviewer to draw him out, though she softened her approach. "That must be fascinating. I noticed a reef close to shore when we were driving to the hotel. It's probably teeming with exotic tropical fish. I wish I had snorkeling gear."

Peter smiled. "Where did a Chicago girl like you learn to snorkel?"

She gave him a sheepish look. "In a friend's pool, I'm afraid. But I'm a very good swimmer."

"Of course, you know you can rent equipment here at the hotel. But that won't be necessary. I'm off tomorrow, and if Nana doesn't mind, I'd be glad to act as your guide on a trip to Buck Island. I have all the equipment you'll need."

Crista glanced at her friend from the plane.

"After her trip, Nana would be very glad to sleep late and have a leisurely breakfast," Mamie Vandervelt said.

Waiting in the wings until Crista had said good-night to her new friends, Phil followed her to her room. He called softly to her from beneath her balcony. Torn between exasperation and guilt over what she was contemplating, she tried to ignore him. But at last she couldn't stand it anymore.

"Okay, what is it?" she asked, appearing at the railing in her semisheer nightgown and robe.

"I just wanted you to know why I followed you down here," Phil answered, thinking how lovely she looked.

"Well? Why *did* you?" she demanded.

"Because I care about you. I hope to stop you from doing something you'll be sorry for."

For a moment they simply looked at each other. He's so special and I love him so, Crista thought. I don't want to lose him. If only he'd make love to me, I know he'd want us to spend the rest of our lives together.

"Have you changed your mind?" she asked.

"No. But..."

It wasn't in her nature to beg. "Neither have I!" she said. "Don't say you didn't have your chance!"

Seconds later, the curtains to her room shut with a snap, leaving him alone on the palm-fringed sand beneath a vagrant moon. Hell, he thought. If they've delivered my mattress, I may as well get some rest. But he doubted if he'd actually sleep very much. His stay on St. Croix promised to be the pits—if his first night on the island was any indication.

Chapter Six

Punching her pillow into shape, Crista wondered if she'd ever fall asleep. Peter Vandervelt was a decent, clean-cut guy—exactly the type she'd be interested in if she hadn't fallen for Phil. Now she was planning to use Peter to accomplish her own selfish purposes. It made her feel cheap.

Phil's insufferable high-handedness and the meddlesome spirit that had prompted him to follow her all the way to the Caribbean buttressed her determination. Thanks to him, she felt she *had* to carry out her plans. If she didn't, she'd lose her self-respect.

She must have dozed off finally, because her next conscious thought was of the sunlight peeking in under the curtains. My God, what time is it? she asked herself with a start, sitting up and groping about on the nightstand for her watch. I'm supposed to meet Peter at eight-thirty.

Luckily it was just seven forty-five. If she hurried, there'd be time for coffee and orange juice. Pulling back the curtains from the sliding glass doors that led to her balcony, she gazed out at clusters of unripe coconuts hanging among graceful green and yellow fronds, a sea striated in shades of deep blue and brilliant turquoise. A small yellow-and-black bird hopped on the railing, looking for crumbs. Unlike the stiff, icy winds that whistled through the canyons between Chicago's skyscrapers in winter, the breeze off the water was balmy and gentle. It was going to be a gorgeous day.

Deciding to go for broke, Crista donned her minimal yellow bikini under a concealing T-shirt and shorts. *Thank God for the hours I spent last week under Laurin's sunlamp*, she thought. *At least I won't look like I crawled out from under a rock.* But even with a good start on her tan, she knew she'd have to use a powerful sun block on her skin for the first few days.

Peter was waiting for her in the lobby. "Ready for a great time?" he asked with a smile, settling her in his aging Volkswagen convertible. "The underwater trail over Buck Island Reef is famous. Though quite a bit of the coral has been damaged from too much handling, the fish are really something to see. And it's an easy swim. I decided to take you on an excursion boat for your first trip."

She didn't notice that Phil had followed them in his rental minijeep as they had pulled out onto the highway and headed for town. He caught up with them at the harbor, where he managed to wangle a place on their boat for the half-day jaunt.

Furious at the imposition, Crista made up her mind to ignore him altogether.

But Peter wouldn't let her.

"Who's that guy watching you?" he asked as the boat's engines started up, churning the water beside the wharf.

"Somebody I work with back home," Crista admitted, trying to shrug off the question.

"Should we ask him to join us?"

"I'd rather not, if you don't mind. We've...um, dated a little. It's an awkward situation."

Peter grinned. "Enough said. Let's go over the mechanics for a moment. I presume you remember that you need to wet your flippers before you put them on. And spit into your mask so it won't fog up in the water."

They were barely outside the sailboat-dotted harbor when a rain shower blew up with all the brisk intensity so typical at that latitude.

"Don't worry," Peter assured her. "These things never last. It'll be sunny by the time we arrive."

Brief though it was, the shower whipped up some strong winds and choppy waves. As a result their passage out to Buck Island was rough. The tublike excursion boat pitched and rolled.

Though its motion didn't seem to bother Crista, by the time they'd reached their destination several of the other passengers, including Phil, were feeling seasick. An ace at most winter sports, Phil wasn't much of a swimmer. He'd never snorkeled in his life.

As the captain cut the boat's engines and they anchored off the hilly green shape of Buck Island a short distance from the reef, Phil wondered if he'd taken on more than he could handle. But he couldn't let Crista and her new swain get the best of him. Gamely he donned mask, snorkel and fins.

"We're going to swim over to the reef in groups of six," one of the female guides announced. "I'll be leading the first group with this ring buoy in tow in case anybody gets a cramp. Expert swimmers and people who have snorkeled before, off the boat first, please."

"That's us," Peter told Crista, eyeing her trim, bikini-clad figure appreciatively as she took off her shirt. "Down you go."

Thanks to the extensive swimming lessons she'd had as a child, Crista slipped confidently into the turquoise water. It was as clear as glass. With a splash, Peter was beside her. She didn't expect Phil to follow them. From what he'd told her, he belonged with the rank beginners.

She should have known he'd refuse to stay behind.

His flipper-clad feet awkward on the rungs, he stepped off the ladder with trepidation. He was immediately rewarded by a mouthful of salt water, swallowed through his submerged breathing tube. Nobody had taught him the easy technique for blowing the water out. A film of moisture clouded his mask as he sputtered to the surface, gasping for breath.

Before Phil could get acclimated, they were off to the reef. A natural athlete, he found it easier than he'd expected to swim with his face down in the water and breathe through a mouthpiece. But even the gentle rocking, lapping motion of the water against his body increased his queasiness and he couldn't appreciate the beauty of his surroundings very much. He hoped the reef tour would be over as quickly as possible.

Despite her worries over Phil, Crista was enjoying herself. The reef, with its huge, branched racks of elkhorn coral, intricately patterned brain-coral mounds and gracefully waving sea fans, was magnificent—even though, as Peter had warned her, much of its original living color had faded to a bony white.

The fish who frequented its labyrinth of exotic shapes compensated with their rainbow hues. To her delight, Crista recognized many of the species Peter had pointed out to her on the chart behind the excursion boat's little bar. She gazed excitedly at myriad schools of black-and-white-banded butterfly fish, which looked like herds of miniature zebras. Several placid-looking blue parrot-fish brushed by close beside her. A queen angelfish with gaudy blue, green and gold scales stared at her with an expression of perpetual surprise.

Purplish blue tangs, resembling oversize minnows that had bathed in a vat of dye, darted back and forth among polyps of finger coral. Glinting like silver in the filtered light, a barracuda flashed through a crevice in the reef and was gone.

If only she and Phil could be sharing this experience together!

Swimming at Peter's side and taking care not to touch any of the sharp, possibly stinging coral formations, Crista suddenly realized that Phil had fallen a short way behind. Was he all right? Deliberately slowing her pace, she dropped back to check on him.

He's so terrific-looking in his swimming trunks—just the way I imagined him, she thought fondly, waving a tentative hello and pointing to a school of bluehead wrasses. *I love his big shoulders, the dark, curly triangle of chest hair that disappears beneath his waistband and that lean, hard-looking midsection. He has the most muscular, beautifully developed thighs.*

Aware of her gaze, Phil didn't reciprocate with even a glimmer of sensual interest. *Why did you have to lure me down here to this underwater paradise?* his eyes complained as they met hers through the fogged, moisture-beaded window of his mask. *We could be back in Chicago, going to a basketball game or something.*

Crista had a pretty good idea what was going through his mind. *It's because I care about you that I'm doing this, you big jerk,* she retorted silently. *Things could have been different if you'd let them. And anyway, who asked you to come along?*

With a shrug, she rejoined Peter, vowing not to take pity on Phil again.

Most of their party was in a relaxed, even ebullient mood when they returned to the boat. As they started back toward Christiansted, crew members busied themselves behind the bar, whirring tropical drinks in the blender. The sun had come out full force and reggae music was playing on the radio.

Just the thought of drinking anything with rum in it made Phil feel green around the gills. Handing in his borrowed fins and mask to one of the crew members, he wrapped himself in an oversize beach towel and stretched out on one of the benches. The boat was still rolling far too much for his liking. Wishing he could hang his head over the rail and part company with his breakfast, he closed his eyes.

Apparently he *looked* green, too. Despite the way she'd abandoned him so abruptly out on the reef, Crista had begun to worry about him again.

"Phil?" she asked tentatively, resting one hand on his shoulder.

"Can I get you anything, old man?" Peter added, compounding injury with charitable insult. "If you don't want alcohol, how about a fruit juice instead?"

Opening his eyes a crack, Phil regarded the green-eyed mermaid who had transformed his relatively peaceful existence into a physical and emotional nightmare. She looked extraordinarily vibrant and attractive in her yellow bikini, and he didn't doubt for a minute that Peter Vandervelt thought so, too. Half of him longed to tell his rival to shove off and assert that Crista belonged to him.

The other half refused to give her the satisfaction. Both halves felt too rotten to argue the point.

"Nothing ails me that being on dry land won't cure," he muttered, shutting his eyes again. "Thanks anyway. Enjoy yourselves."

Phil wasn't able to do anything more than stagger to a bench in the shade of a tamarind tree beside the harbor when they returned to port. Realizing he'd given up any idea of following them, Crista felt a moment of panic. Did she really want to carry out her scheme and seduce Peter when she was in love with Phil?

Well, what choice do I have? she asked herself. He won't make love to me. And until he does, our relationship isn't going anywhere. I have to go ahead, for both our sakes.

She and Peter had lunch at the King's Alley Café, a small, open-air spot with plastic tablecloths and a tree-shaded view of the harbor. Birds chirped in the overgrown foliage along the cobbled, shop-lined passageway. Striving to bolster her courage, Crista half hoped Phil might appear on the scene.

But he didn't.

"Where to?" Peter asked after they'd finished their curried chicken salad and he'd paid the check. "Shopping? A few hours at the beach? Or a tour of the lab where I work? Nana said not to disturb her until three."

Crista struggled with her conscience, suddenly tempted to forget the whole purpose of her visit. But with Phil out of commission and Peter's grandmother safely relaxing in her suite, she knew she'd been granted the perfect opportunity to achieve her goal.

"Let's go back to the beach at the hotel," she suggested in a small voice. "I have some piña colada mix in the refrigerator. We can stop off at my room for a drink."

During the twenty-minute ride back to the Crescent Beach over tortuous roads and green, hump-backed hills dotted with the ruins of sugar plantations, she became progressively more tense. Now that I'm really at the point of doing something about it, she thought, I don't know if I can carry out my threat.

"What's wrong?" Peter asked as they entered her room. "You're as nervous as a cat. I'm not planning to tear your clothes off, if that's what you think."

Crista jumped as if he'd read her mind. She turned to him with an agonized expression. "Actually," she admitted, "that's just what I was going to ask you to do...."

For a moment Peter looked at her as if he couldn't quite believe his ears. "You're kidding, of course," he responded uncertainly. "*Aren't* you?"

"No. I'm dead serious."

Meeting his eyes with difficulty, Crista realized she'd have to explain. But only the minimum, she thought. Choosing her words with care and more embarrassed than she'd ever been in her life, she recounted her problems as an innocent in a world where everyone went to bed on the third date. She also told him about the column, though she didn't mention her connection with its author.

"Right after the column came out, I fell hard for a particular guy," she admitted. "I don't think it's stretching the truth to say that he felt the same. But he's got a thing against marriage. He feels that if he took me to bed he'd have to marry me. I came down here to the Virgin Islands with the express purpose of making my virginity a nonissue between us."

Obviously stunned, Peter didn't say a word.

"I know it's asking a lot," Crista added, willing him not to walk out the door. "But I like you, Peter. I'd be very honored and grateful if you'd consider helping me with this."

"You mean... *initiate you into sex*?"

Swallowing, she nodded.

He shook his head. "Now I've heard it all."

They stared at each other in mutual consternation.

"I realize my request is a bit unorthodox," she acknowledged after a moment. "But would you please think it over while I fix us those drinks?"

Nervously she got out the makings for piña coladas. Mixing them in disposable plastic glasses, she handed one to Peter.

"Thanks," he said in a strained voice, taking a healthy gulp of his drink. Crista did likewise. For a moment neither of them said anything.

"I like you too, Crista," Peter told her at last. "Very much. But I'm afraid I have to disappoint you. What you're proposing... just isn't right."

His resistance only stiffened her resolve. "Why not?" she insisted, trying to forget her feelings for Phil. "Aren't I attractive to you? Can you honestly say it didn't cross your mind that we might have an affair?"

"What if it did?" Peter grimaced, clearly uncomfortable at being forced to admit the truth.

Gently she took his drink from his hand and set it beside hers on the dresser. "Please don't feel I think any the less of you for that," she said earnestly. "You're a very attractive man, exactly the kind I'd have fallen for if I hadn't met... that other guy first. Surely that counts for something."

He shrugged. "Maybe."

"Of course it does. I realize we've only known each other a short time. But I feel we're friends. If it isn't you, it's going to be somebody else."

"Oh, hell. If you put it like that..."

His resistance crumbling, Peter agreed to try, though he warned her it might result in an awkward situation. "Making love to order, particularly when I know you care about another man, isn't very conducive to passion," he said. "I assume you realize men can't always perform on demand."

He had just taken her in his arms and begun kissing her experimentally on the mouth when Phil's head appeared at the balcony railing.

"Unhand that woman at once!" Phil shouted, looking and sounding like the hero of a B movie as he hoisted himself up and climbed over.

"Oh, nooooo!" Crista moaned. "Tell me this isn't happening!"

"Who the heck *are* you, anyway?" Peter demanded, keeping one arm around her. "Crista says you're a colleague. You act more like a bodyguard. Or a nosy little brother!"

Every instinct urged Phil to punch out the good-looking man whose tanned, lean fingers were curled so protectively around Crista's waist. But he wasn't sure she'd ever forgive him. Besides, he was still feeling pretty rocky. And—barring some statement of intent on his part—he didn't have the right.

Secretly relieved at his intervention, Crista whispered in Peter's ear, "Maybe you'd better go and let me deal with this."

Oh, his look told her. So *he*'s the one.

"Okay, Crista," he said, giving Phil an exasperated glance. "You know where to reach me if you change your mind."

With Peter gone, Crista wanted to excoriate Phil for trying to run her life. But she couldn't find the right words.

She'd felt an enormous surge of respite when he'd appeared, and honesty wouldn't let her deny it.

For his part, Phil felt sheepish—as if he'd behaved like a buffoon. But that didn't stop him from lecturing her on the hazards of getting involved with a stranger.

"Don't you know you could catch some terrible disease, let alone damage your psyche permanently by going against your most cherished principles?" he asked.

Crista made an impudent face. "Give me credit for a little sense," she countered. "I had protection. And Peter Vandervelt is an extremely clean-cut guy. You and I didn't know each other, either, until a few weeks ago. Yet you were on the verge of taking me to bed!"

He had to admit there was merit in what she said.

"Look," he suggested, seeking to smooth over the situation. "I've messed up your plans. What do you say we stretch out on the beach for a while? And then go into town? I'll take you to dinner and a show."

Unwilling to dwell too much on the unreasoning happiness she felt, just being invited to spend time in his company, Crista agreed. They selected two chaise longues close to the edge of the water, his in direct sun and hers positioned in light shade.

With so many unresolved issues between them, it wasn't surprising they had so little to say to each other. Meanwhile, Phil's proximity and relative state of undress were giving Crista fits. With all her being, she longed to reach out and stroke the corded muscles of his upper arms, run her palms over his powerful shoulders and muscular thighs. What heaven it would be, she thought, just to tangle my fingers in his chest hair, lie beneath his body. The black swimming trunks he wore hinted all too clearly at the generosity of his manhood.

I mustn't let him get to me like this, Crista swore, battling to exhibit some self-control. Not unless he's willing to give me what we both want so much. Resolutely she turned over on her stomach. After twenty minutes or so of deliberate relaxation, she managed to drop off to sleep.

Lying beside her, Phil found it was all he could do to keep from resting his hand on the trim derriere that was revealed by her scant bikini bottom. The smooth line of her back and slender waist positively cried out to be touched. Shutting his eyes, he resisted the impulse to lift her shining cap of hair and place a tender kiss on the nape of her neck.

What's the matter with you? he railed at himself. You've never held back like this with anyone. Before Crista, you hadn't met the woman who could cause you to hesitate.

You never followed a woman halfway to South America, either, a voice inside him reminded. Ask yourself a few questions about that.

When she awoke, palm fronds were shading Crista's chair. Beside her, Phil's place was empty. The stab of abandonment she felt eased when she saw him returning from the bar area with two drinks in his hands.

"Orange juice for you, milk for me," he said ruefully. "The old stomach's still accepting contributions under protest."

They separated briefly, adjourning to their rooms to shower and change. Intoxicated by the idea that Phil might be on the brink of relenting, Crista selected a backless sundress in magenta cotton that accentuated the mahogany highlights in her hair. With a careful hand, she applied her makeup the way the counter girl at the department store had taught her and piled on several strands of exotic-looking wood-and-crystal beads. To her surprise, the result was like something out of a magazine.

Phil knocked at her door dressed Don Johnson-style in a casual white sport coat, pink Henley shirt and pale gray cotton trousers. His unruly dark hair was freshly washed and he smelled wonderful, like a tangy breeze with a hint of lime in it.

"You look fabulous!" he told her with unabashed pleasure, taking her hands in his and looking as if he wanted to ravage her mouth. "Just remember that you're *my* date."

Parking the minijeep in the lot near the harbor and the King Christian Hotel, Phil led her down quaint, cobbled Strandgate Alley to the Tivoli Gardens, a second-story, open-air restaurant. Apparently St. Croix residents and visitors alike tended to eat late, because they were among the Tivoli's first customers of the evening.

A smiling waiter led them to a table for two beside the railing that overlooked the street. Sparkling lights were strung through a jungle of tropical plants. They also outlined the arches that supported the ceiling. Hurricane lamps placed on the tables flickered softly as the sky settled into twilight.

From the pavement below, the chatter of shopkeepers heading home from work and tourists just going out for the evening floated up to them. A blend of several types of music drifted in their direction from the Moonraker Hotel bar and the Calabash Supper Club across the street.

"That's the nightclub where I plan to take you later," Phil said, nodding toward the Calabash as Crista savored her curried Thai shrimp and cucumber salad. "Dr. Hoodoo is scheduled to perform tonight. The concierge at the hotel said it was a terrific show."

Following dinner, which for Phil had consisted of a bland chicken dish and rice, they held hands as they crossed to the Calabash and ascended its narrow stairway.

The breeze-swept upper deck with its white plastic chairs, umbrellas and tentlike awnings looked extremely informal for a nightclub, and Crista wondered if Phil had misunderstood. A buffet of Caribbean-style food was laid out on a steam table and a number of children were present, eating dinner with their parents. One small girl had wandered up to what appeared to be a small dance floor. She gyrated rhythmically and unself-consciously to the music of a calypso band. Smiling at her, a woman in a batik sarong led them to a ringside seat.

Gradually the crowd changed as the sky deepened to black and show time neared. Though some of the families remained, most of the newcomers were couples. Many looked as if they were on their honeymoon. I wish *we* were, Crista thought.

At last Dr. Hoodoo came out to a thunderous round of applause. A barrel-chested black man in his late forties or early fifties, he was naked to the waist. Below it, he was dressed in a sequined loincloth and what looked like black bicycling tights decorated with gold fringe below the knees. He wore sequined armbands, a heavy gold neck collar and feathers in his hair. His large, dusty-looking feet were bare.

Moving about the dance-floor area to the calypso music, he lit a three-pronged torch. He made a great show of passing it up and down his arms and around his torso before putting out the fire with his mouth. Then, throwing back his head, he blew out a little tongue of flame. A second wave of applause erupted.

Before proceeding to his next trick, Dr. Hoodoo chatted with the audience. He asked the evening's crop of honeymooners to raise their hands.

"What about you two?" he asked Phil and Crista, turning abruptly to them. "I didn't see any hands go up at this table. Are you married? Or living in sin?"

"Neither.... We're friends," Phil hastened to answer, clearly embarrassed to be the center of attention.

"Pretty good friends from the looks of things," Dr. Hoodoo said with a laugh, playing to the crowd. "Better hurry up and see the preacher. Every mon needs a wife."

Not daring to meet Phil's eyes, Crista felt as if the outspoken performer's flaming torches had lightly brushed *her* cheeks.

Chapter Seven

In preparation for his next act, Dr. Hoodoo laid out a square black cloth on the dance floor and brought forth a cardboard box of empty liquor bottles still aromatic from their former contents. With a hammer and a great deal of fanfare, he smashed the bottles to smithereens. That finished, he spread out the jagged shards on the cloth at his feet. People in the back rows crowded forward for a better look.

"The Lord Voodoo willing, I plan to walk on this broken glass, ladies and gentlemen," he announced. "Even to dance on it. Is everybody all right? Some of you don't look so good. I'm getting a little scared, just looking at your faces."

A wave of nervous laughter swept to the rooftop. Murmuring what he called a "voodoo prayer," the intrepid performer circled the cloth several times, testing the glass gingerly with his toes. Suddenly he stepped onto the sharp glass fragments. They crunched audibly beneath his bare soles.

An "ooooooooooooh" of astonishment rose from the audience. Appalled, Crista hid her face against Phil's shoulder.

"It's okay to look.... He's not even bleeding," Phil whispered.

To everyone's horrified fascination, the voodoo performer stomped on the glass and jumped up in the air, landing on the broken pieces with all his weight. True to his word, he danced about on it. There wasn't a sign of injury.

"The Lord Voodoo taught me to do this, and I will teach you," he offered. "I need three volunteers, preferably over six feet tall or one hundred eighty pounds. We have to put my magic to the test."

As might have been expected, few members of the audience were forthcoming. One lady in a print dress who looked as if she weighed at least two hundred pounds hesitantly agreed.

"Have it your way," Dr. Hoodoo said with a shrug, grabbing Phil and another man by the sleeves. "We'll use draftees instead."

Never one to enjoy being in front of a crowd, and definitely unwilling to walk on broken glass, Phil shuffled reluctantly to center stage while Crista held her breath. I'll be okay if I keep my loafers on, he thought. Unfortunately, Dr. Hoodoo's first command to his newly recruited assistants was to remove their shoes. The other participants obeyed and slowly Phil followed suit, shamed into cooperating.

"Ready?" Dr. Hoodoo asked. The electric guitar and steel drum played a few anticipatory bars.

"I'm not so sure," the hefty woman replied with a tense giggle, staring at the glittering glass fragments.

Ending the suspense, Dr. Hoodoo stretched out on his back atop the broken glass. "You three walk over my stomach," he instructed, eliciting a wave of relief from Phil. "I'll make a bridge for you. See how easy it is?"

Dr. Hoodoo emerged from the demonstration unscathed. So did Phil. Crista couldn't resist throwing her arms around him when he returned to their table.

"You were so brave just to go up there at all!" she exclaimed. "I would have been petrified."

Following a short intermission, Dr. Hoodoo returned with his limbo show. A contest was organized involving more audience participation. It had barely begun when the power went out. Around them, the city was cloaked in a velvety blackness. A few lights came on here and there, powered by generators or flaring from the wicks of hurricane lamps. Casually, as if power failures were an everyday occurrence, several Calabash employees came forward with torches to light the stage.

Instinctively Phil put his arm around Crista's shoulders in the flickering half-light. "Would you like to go?" he asked.

"Maybe we should," she answered. "Do you think we'll be able to find our way in the dark?"

Hand in hand, they stumbled out, feeling their way inch by inch down the unfamiliar steps. Though Christiansted's narrow streets loomed eerie with shadows, a full moon shone overhead, riding like a seventeenth-century Spanish galleon among the trade-wind clouds. Crista felt nurtured and cared for as Phil's arm tightly encircled her waist. Like a cavalier of the old school, he warned her to step down or up, as required by the worn, uneven pavement.

Finally they were back at his rented jeep. "We're a long way from Michigan Avenue and the *Tribune* offices, aren't we?" he asked, brushing her lips with his.

A stab of longing raced through Crista's body. The best part of that was finding themselves together. "Yes, a very long way," she said.

In the jeep, she laid her head on his shoulder. With a sigh of contentment she cuddled against him as they drove out of town into the wooded scrub of the outlying districts. How wonderful it felt, just to relax into his keeping like this.

If only the barriers that separate us would disappear and we could merge in total abandon, she thought. I don't have the slightest doubt that it would change the course of our lives. Though she didn't know much about sex, she could imagine how it would be between her and Phil. In her every daydream since they'd met, their coming together had been soul-shattering, transcendent.

If we do make love, the earth will move just as it does in novels and movies, she told herself.

Outside her room, Phil was reluctant to say good-night. "Why don't we wander down to the beach for a while?" he suggested. "It's a splendid night, soft and full of promise. I'd like us to spend a little more of it together."

Their arms about each other, they started down the crushed-coral walk, kicking off their shoes when they reached the sand. Overhead, the moon was high and full, a silent, expectant presence waiting for him to take her fully into his embrace.

Under the shadowy palms, accompanied by the insistent *hush-hush* of the surf, it happened. The kiss that drew them together had been trembling on the lip of desire all evening. And the magic it contained was far more powerful than that in any voodoo performer's bag of tricks.

Bluntly yet with infinite tenderness, he claimed her mouth. Starved for his touch, her lips parted to receive him. For a tremulous moment their breaths met and mingled. Then he was pushing his way inside, his tongue dueling with hers as if he would plunder her very depths.

One of his strong, capable hands tangled in the hair at her nape, tilting her head backward so that he could gain even deeper access. The other gripped the soft flesh of her buttocks through the rumpled skirt of her dress, branding her with the emblem of his need.

Never—not even by Phil—had Crista been kissed that way. Never had she longed to give a man so much, *take* so much from him in return. A white-hot flame of certainty arose in her, searing the most private places of her being and opening them to his access. This was the time and place, she knew; *this* was the man she would love forever. She wanted to offer him everything she had, everything she was.

Phil felt as if he were drowning in his ache for her. The passionate, delicious taste of her mouth, the sweet thrust of her lower body against his, were almost more than he could bear. He wanted to uncover her breasts and lave their nipples into tight submission, bury himself in the warm, wet wilderness between her thighs.

Crista, he thought. Sweet Crista! I want to surround you, immerse myself in you, become part of you. With every breath we take, I long to ravage you more. Every impulse in my blood is begging me to take you, to pull you down with me on the sand and cover you with my body.

It was what she wanted, too. He knew it, felt it—just as he knew he couldn't let himself be swayed by her desire. Deep within the outpouring of his hunger, like a diamond hidden in an avalanche of rubies, was something new in his sexual universe—the urge to nurture and protect.

He had felt it at least once before, when he'd come so close to making love to her at his apartment. He'd known then, too, that to take from her without giving back some essential part of himself would be a mistake.

Crista's thoughts were wrapped up in desire. "Phil," she pleaded, the admission of her craving wrung from her as she burrowed against him. "I need you so desperately. Please... don't turn me away again."

For a moment he simply held her, his face buried against her neck as he gathered strength. She was going to be furious with him, maybe even hate him for this.

"I can't, sweetheart," he acknowledged, every word twisting in his gut. "I *want* to—more than you can guess. But I have a responsibility...."

Stunned by what she perceived as the unmitigated cruelty of his actions, Crista stared at him in disbelief. Oh, yes—you want to, she thought bitterly. Just not enough to risk the kind of commitment I'm ready to give you with all my heart.

Fiercely she longed to strike out at him and wound him in return. Her eyes blazed in the silvery, dappled light.

"Guess what you can do with your precious responsibility," she cried, wrenching away from him with all her strength. "That's right.... Shove it where it'll cause you the most discomfort! Henceforth, keep your grubby hands off my vacation or I'll have you arrested!"

Scooping up her sandals in midflight, she raced away from him in the general direction of her room. I hope he's awake all night, she thought indignantly, inserting her key into the lock. Because I don't expect to sleep a wink.

Left behind on the beach, Phil was suffering an agony of regret. But though he yearned to run after her and beg her to let him share her bed, he didn't budge from the spot. If he dared to accept what she was offering, he'd hold himself accountable. He'd feel a strong obligation to marry her. He didn't stop to examine the fact that the idea wasn't quite as repugnant to him as it had at first seemed.

Crista awoke late the next morning with a dull headache behind her eyes. Her mind still fogged with sleep, she cast about vaguely for the cause of her distress. A moment later, recalling the ruin of what had promised to be the evening of a lifetime, she groaned, took two aspirin and closed her eyes again. It was nearly ten before she roused herself sufficiently to shower and dress.

What now? she asked herself, swigging a soda from her room's minirefrigerator rather than go down for coffee and perhaps encounter Phil. I can hardly call up Peter and tell him I'd like to resume where we left off. That really *would* be using him.

Yet she didn't want her trip to be a total waste. Glancing at the schedule posted on her dresser, she saw that the hotel shuttle would be leaving for town within five or ten minutes. I might as well go in—see the sights and do some shopping, she decided, shouldering her camera and purse. I have to buy something for Gran anyway.

As he had the day before, Phil lounged in his minijeep, reading the morning newspaper and waited for Crista to emerge. When he saw her aboard the shuttle van, he took his time pulling out behind it. He didn't want her voicing a complaint.

Twenty minutes later, the shuttle driver let off his passengers near the post office, at the east end of town. Across a little park, Fort Christiansvaern—built by the Danish in 1749 to guard the harbor and the Danish West India and Guinea Company's warehouses from pirates—glowed yellow and cream in the morning light. Guess I'll tour it and the other historic buildings, maybe write an article for the *Tribune*'s travel section, Crista thought. There'll be plenty of time for shopping after lunch.

She didn't see Phil shadowing her footsteps as she paid her admission at the little bookstore and rangers' station just inside the gate. He'd taken care to keep well out of sight behind a honeymoon couple and a local family with three children. Like some nefarious character hiding out from the police, he ducked into the gloom cast by the venerable tabby cement and brick archways as Crista looked about the fort's prison area, photographing a bright branch of royal poinciana blossoms through the bars of a long-abandoned cell.

But he couldn't resist approaching her when she climbed the smoothly worn steps to the battlements and stood looking out over the harbor beside jauntily painted cannons and flags snapping in the breeze. Caution couldn't stop him from trying to set things straight with her, though he wasn't quite sure how that could be achieved.

She frowned as she caught sight of his lean, powerful figure and windblown hair. "What do you think you're doing?" she demanded. "I thought I told you last night... *Stay away from me!*"

"Crista..."

Hoping no one would pay any attention to them, he caught her by the hand. Immediately she pulled away from him.

"You know you don't really mean that," he said.

She gave him an incredulous look. "Are you crazy or something? I'd dive off these battlements if I didn't think you'd follow."

Turning on her heel, she strolled to the fort's northwest bastion and adjusted the exposure on her camera for a shot of the harbor. Below, yachts floated at anchor in a bay of transparent turquoise. The only shadows were made by passing frigate birds and clouds.

Catching sight of a notebook peeking out of her trouser pocket, Phil guessed she'd decided to write a travel piece. Good idea, he thought. I should be doing the same thing. But his heart wasn't in it—not with so much bad feeling between them. Too bad they couldn't be researching an article together.

To his chagrin, he imagined himself a puppy dog as he trailed her from the fort to the Old Danish Customs House, the Steeple Building with its prominent cupola and clock, and on past the trimly painted layer cake of Government House to the historic house of worship known as Our Lord of Saboth Church. She had just turned into the church's ancient courtyard when a shower blew up as it had the day before.

Together they ducked beneath the sheltering branches of a huge gumbo-limbo tree. Rain spattered like bullets on the aged stones as sunlight continued to filter through the leaves.

"Crista," said Phil. "Have lunch with me. Let me make it up to you."

"You couldn't—not in a million years!" Determinedly she extracted the rain bonnet Gran had given her from her purse.

Crista lunched on a sandwich and a bottled pineapple drink in another courtyard off Company Street while Phil lounged at a nearby table. I've got to lose him, she thought. He's ruining everything. I can't even concentrate on my article, let alone the reason I came to the Virgin Islands in the first place.

Maybe shopping would do the trick. Men were notoriously bored by trooping through store after store as their female companions browsed among perfumes, expensive jewelry and fashionable clothing. She had nothing to lose but her money by giving it a try.

I know, she thought. I'll look up that friend of Bunny Sharpe's who manages the shop specializing in South American emeralds. As the *Tribune*'s longtime society editor, Bunny knew a lot of people in a lot of places. She'd urged Crista to look up Nick Danzen when she got to Christiansted.

Crista found Danzen's shop—designated Bijoux Verts, in gold letters on snappy green awnings—below the Calabash Supper Club where she and Phil had been the night before. Not bothering to glance over her shoulder to see if he was still following her, she went inside. The vast array of emeralds and numerous other gems set in gold and platinum took her breath away.

Forgetting her purpose, she edged slowly along one of the glass-and-mahogany counters, eyeing the glittering green stones in their fabulous settings. She hardly noticed Phil trying to appear inconspicuous in the shop's entryway, or the man in his early forties who had come to stand opposite her.

"May I help you, miss?" the man asked in a distinctly Danish accent.

She gazed into blue eyes with rather attractive crinkles at the corners set in a lean, tanned, not bad-looking face. Smiling at her across the counter, the man had a rakish grin and touches of gray at the temples. Medium tall and compact of build in his tropical-weight suit, he was impeccably groomed.

"Thanks," she answered. "But I'm just browsing. You wouldn't happen to know if Nick Danzen is around, would you? A friend of mine in Chicago, Bunny Sharpe, told me I should look him up."

The rakish grin broadened as he surveyed her from head to toe. "*I*'m Nick Danzen," he said.

To her surprise, Bunny had taken the trouble to write to Nick that Crista would be on St. Croix. "I'm stuck in the shop until four," he said. "And unfortunately I've scheduled myself to work tonight. In between, why don't we have a drink? We could meet at the Bombay Club."

Unaware that she now had a date, Phil traipsed determinedly after Crista as she allowed her most perverse shopping spirit free rein. There weren't many boutiques along King Street, Strand Street or in the Pan Am Pavilion that she hadn't visited by the time four o'clock approached. She felt a certain grim satisfaction when she noted Phil's dragging footsteps.

He was slightly puzzled when she entered the Bombay nightclub, walking past the floppy old ceiling fans in the open-air patio and into the bar area. Through a screened partition, he watched her slide onto a barstool.

Crista's not the sort to pick up a one-night stand in a place like this, he told himself. I know her better than that. So what's she doing here? Just thirsty?

Several seconds passed before he realized she wasn't alone. Seated on the stool next to hers, a sophisticated-looking, middle-aged man was paying for her daiquiri. A moment later, the two of them picked up their drinks and walked toward the back of the bar.

Jealously sensing a new threat to his peace of mind and Crista's virtue, Phil followed her inside. The bar's cozy, quaint decor—a potpourri of dark wood, green plants, framed wine labels and various posters including one of John Lennon—reminded Phil of several neighborhood hangouts he'd known on Chicago's North Side. Working his way along the bar, he appropriated a stool at the far corner and ordered himself a beer.

Even though he craned his neck, he couldn't see much more than the top of Crista's head over the back of her booth, plus an occasional gesture by the man seated opposite her. Any attempt on his part to overhear their conversation was frustrated by the raucous beat emanating from a jukebox. Thinking murderous thoughts, he sipped his beer in disgust.

Listening as Nick described everyday life on St. Croix, Crista found him something of a smoothie, though a genuinely nice guy. He wasn't as intense, funny, sexy or talented as Phil. But it was a safe bet he was more experienced than Peter. He had a certain flair she couldn't quite define. She instinctively liked the way he took himself less than seriously. Maybe he'd turn out to be the "guide" figure she was looking for.

Nick ordered a second round of drinks. When they'd finished them, he offered to drive her back to her hotel.

"As shop manager, I can afford to be a little late," he said. "You've probably missed the last shuttle out to the east end, and a cab can be rather expensive."

On their way back to Grapetree Bay in his Porsche, Crista's new acquaintance invited her to attend a party with him the following evening.

"It's going to be held at a home built around the ruins of an old sugar mill," he said. "It's quite a showplace. The hostess, Laura Bettendorf, is my good friend and something of a character. Her parties attract most of the local literati and visiting celebrities."

Back at the Bombay Club, Crista had wished mightily that Phil would interrupt their tête-à-tête with a declaration that he'd changed his mind. But it hadn't happened. Anyway, she thought, the party might be fun.

"I'd love to go," she told Nick with a smile.

She didn't object when he gave her a light but thoroughly expressive goodbye kiss.

Parked behind a hibiscus hedge near the entrance to her room, Phil watched the entire interchange. He began to feel slightly desperate. *I get rid of one guy and she immediately finds another one,* he thought. *There are probably hundreds of them waiting in the wings.*

No sooner had Nick left than Phil was knocking on Crista's door.

"What do you want?" she demanded irritably, hairbrush in hand. "I thought I told you..."

"Just to have a drink with you," he answered with unexpected humility. "Please, Crista... I won't try to talk you into or out of anything. There are positively no strings attached."

He didn't mention having seen her with another man.

Still angry at him for refusing to make love to her the night before, Crista couldn't help being aware of the devotion Phil had exhibited by following her throughout such a long and exhausting day. The last thing she wanted at that moment was another drink. But she supposed it wouldn't hurt to have a soft drink with him. Loving him as she did, she couldn't bear to turn down the invitation.

Seated at a table beside the hotel pool, they drank their sodas, saying very little. A calypso group was playing and Phil asked her if she'd like to dance. Moving with him in the informal, breeze-blown setting, she realized more than ever how much he meant to her.

I don't want to make love to anyone else but you, she confessed silently, resisting the urge to snuggle closer in his arms. *The thought of doing that is totally repugnant to me. But if I don't, you and I will never get together. You're so afraid of settling down, you'll continue to back out of any* clinches. I *have* to carry out my plan if we're to have the ghost of a chance.

Reluctantly, she decided to ask Nick Danzen to initiate her into the art of lovemaking.

Chapter Eight

That night, after Phil walked her to her room, Crista called one of the numbers listed on the card atop her hotel dresser and arranged for a tour of the island the next day. The evening she'd just spent with the man she loved, dancing and sipping sodas by the pool while they remained sunk in their private thoughts, had left her in a bittersweet mood. If I don't get out and concentrate on sightseeing tomorrow, she thought, I'll just hang around here with him. My resolve will waver and I'll decide not to go to bed with Nick. Later, I'll have cause for regret.

If Phil hadn't become too discouraged by his long trek through the streets of Christiansted, no doubt he'd follow her. But with sufficient distraction, she could probably weather that.

The following morning Crista was waiting in a white knit top, tropical print skirt and sandals when the tour company's open-air minibus pulled up outside the lobby. Handing over her fare, she took a seat beneath its red-and-white striped awning. She ordered her heart not to skip a beat when Phil got in beside her, edging her over slightly on the narrow bench seat.

"You two newlyweds?" asked a matron of about sixty who was seated just ahead of them. She gave them a complaisant smile.

It was the second time they'd been asked that question in as many days. "No," said Phil, appearing slightly more comfortable with that subject of interrogation. "We're just friends."

The matron's smile vanished. Giving them a disapproving look, she turned her back. She's convinced we're sleeping together, Crista thought with amusement. Well, she couldn't be more wrong. She had to admit that previously, such a misconception would have bothered her a great deal—even on the part of a stranger. Now she wished with all her heart that the woman was right.

There was nothing new to see or think about on the well-worn road between her hotel and downtown Christiansted. Once they'd reached the city's familiar streets, their guide began imparting the history of the buildings, many of which she'd visited the day before. She listened distractedly to his recitation of how crushed stone, molasses and coral had been combined to create thick walls that kept interiors cool while withstanding the ravages of time and hurricanes.

When they headed west toward Frederiksted, the driver pointed out what he fondly referred to as the Miracle Mile, a straggling collection of strip malls featuring fast-food restaurants, as well as various appliance, furniture and grocery stores. As if indoctrinating them for permanent residence, he quoted land prices by the half acre and explained the water situation.

Many people still had their cisterns, he said. But, "Most of the potable water be comin' from the desalinization plant in Christiansted."

Her shoulder aligned with Phil's and her thigh brushing his, Crista was grateful for the barrier of clothing as they jolted over sometimes tortuous roads on their way to the Columbus landing site, botanical garden and Whim Great House, which she was considering as the subject of another travel piece. How different this would be if we *were* on our honeymoon, she thought, letting her imagination run wild against her best intentions. We'd already be so close, nothing could separate us. Sated with each other, we'd be tingling at the thought of our next lovemaking.

With such mental images wreaking havoc on her emotions, Crista didn't object when Phil attached himself to her during their botanical tour. Something of their former easiness returned as they walked beneath huge tamarinds, turpentine trees and mahoganies, sampling the edible fruits of Barbados cherry bushes and inhaling the lush scent of some tropical flower that lay heavily on the air.

Yet, despite the idyllic setting and their temporary accord, Crista's heart ached. Phil was so dear to her now. She loved his unruly hair and light-drenched eyes, his sense of humor, even the shape of his blunt, neatly manicured fingernails. Just his quick flash of smile—brilliant and self-deprecating—was enough now to turn her head. She could feel herself slipping, retreating to a point of indecision where ending her virginity with a stranger was concerned.

Phil asked the guide to take their picture with his camera when they came upon a latticed arch overgrown with tiny white blossoms. Though Crista tried to demur, he wouldn't hear of it.

"Smile for the man, sweetheart," he insisted, putting one arm around her shoulders and drawing her close.

She tried to do as she was bidden, wondering if this would be their most romantic memory of the trip.

Beneath their guide's capable fingers the exposure was set and the shutter clicked. "Okay, that's it," the man said. "You two honeymooners?"

Not again! Crista groaned to herself. "No!" she answered more sharply than she'd intended.

Phil gave her a thoughtful look.

"That's too bad, miss," the man replied, handing back Phil's camera. "You look so happy together. I guess you didn't know this was a wedding bower."

Crista was tight-lipped as they got back aboard the minibus and headed for Estate Whim. For his part, Phil was toying with dangerous notions. Except for his truthful answer to the matronly woman's question at the beginning of their tour, he realized he'd done nothing to disabuse the other passengers of the idea that he and Crista were man and wife.

Maybe marriage wouldn't be so bad if it didn't have to take the form of two harried parents and a houseful of screaming kids, he thought. One man and one woman, career oriented and sharing a life of work, concerts, sporting events, intimate little dinners and weekends in the country—now *that* would be more his style. Unfortunately, Crista wanted a big family like the one he'd been raised in. She'd told him so herself. If only they could compromise!

His mind busily skirted the edge of a precipice he'd avoided for years as they walked through Whim Great House, the centerpiece of a former sugar plantation once owned by St. Croix's Danish governor. Though Crista was taking copious notes, he barely saw the building's round, breezy, antique-furnished living room or elegant dining room full of pink Lustre Wedgwood and blue-and-white china that had arrived on the island as ballast in the hold of some sailing ship.

Crista and I married! he thought. Would it work? Just the idea of saying irrevocable vows gave him the heebie-jeebies. He and the green-eyed sprite who'd caused him so many sleepless nights were very different in the way they'd grown up and what mattered to them. Give them a week and they'd be at each other's throats.

But maybe not. It struck him suddenly as they toured the house's master suite with its pineapple four-poster, coconut-husk mattress and elongated planter's chair that he hadn't been worrying about any exclusivity clause. Since Crista had appeared in his life, he hadn't even thought about other women. Can that be because she's the one? he asked himself.

When they got back to the hotel, he'd ask her to dinner so they could talk it over, he decided, barely noticing the salmon-and-ochre buildings of Fredriksted or the tangle of trees and lush vegetation in the rain forest near St. Croix's northeast coast. It never occurred to him that she might have other plans.

He was dumbfounded, totally crestfallen, when Crista informed him she was spending the evening with Nick.

"He's a good friend of Bunny Sharpe's," she explained as they stood outside her door. "She asked me to look him up...even wrote him I'd be coming. He wants to take me to a party at some swank place built around a sugar mill. I could hardly refuse."

I don't know why not, Phil thought. If you had, we could be spending the evening together. "Where is this place?" he asked.

Too late, Crista realized she'd fallen into a trap. "Never mind," she responded hastily. "I absolutely *forbid* you to follow me there. It would be terribly embarrassing. If you do, I'll never speak to you again."

Phil didn't look cowed in the least. "Tell me the truth," he demanded. "Do you plan to sleep with this guy? Because I absolutely forbid *that*. One look at him, and you can tell he's been around."

Guilt reared its ugly head, though Crista hadn't done anything—yet. Defensively her temper flared. "You have no right to give me orders of any kind!" she averred, fighting the urge to stamp her foot like a child.

The golden flecks in Phil's hazel eyes glittered dangerously. He, too, looked ready to explode. "Is that so?" he answered in a gritty voice, obviously keeping his cool with difficulty. "Have it your way, honey bunch. Just remember... Two can play at that game."

Crista was shaking from their abrasive interchange as he stalked back to his minijeep. He wanted to have dinner with me, to talk, she thought, trembling as she unlocked the door. I wonder what would have been forthcoming? Another lecture on why I shouldn't go through with my plan? Or an admission that he's had a change of heart?

Something about the way he'd stated his invitation had raised a question in her mind. Yet she hadn't been fully aware of it during the heat of their argument. Thanks to their harsh words, the question would go unanswered. Would they ever learn to settle things peaceably between them? Disconsolately, Crista leaned her forehead against the cool glass of her balcony doors before opening them to the late-afternoon breeze and beginning to get ready for her date.

Patting herself dry from her shower, she confronted the question of what to wear. Local literati and visiting celebrities would be attending the Bettendorf woman's party, Nick had said. That could mean anyone from some obscure lecturer on the habits of tropical birds to the hottest new movie star. Maybe some all-time great in the entertainment field would be present. She'd heard Maureen O'Hara had a house on the island.

In any event, she had to look her best. Okay, she told herself, the lion's share of her attention still focused on Phil. You've got two choices.

Both gowns—newly purchased during her spending spree before she left Chicago—were strapless and would emphasize the honeyed tan of her upper bosom and shoulders. The first, with a puckered print top and arrow-straight, full-length white sharkskin skirt that was slit to the thigh, seemed a bit too formal for the occasion. She decided on the second, a little black cotton number with large white polka dots and a layered, ruffled hem that ended several inches above the knee. Banded with hot pink atop its low-cut bodice and on the lower edge of its ruffles, it swirled flirtatiously around her legs.

Fastening on high-heeled sandals in the same shade of hot pink and inserting pearl studs in her earlobes, she evaluated her handiwork in the mirror.

"Not bad for a gawky virgin from Wilmette," she drawled, making a face.

Once she'd declared herself ready, Crista began to get cold feet. Regretting the argument with Phil more with every passing minute, she placed a call to Nick's shop. Frantically her mind ran the gamut of polite and plausible excuses as the phone rang. She had every intention of announcing she couldn't go with him.

Unfortunately, he'd already left. She'd have to attend the party with him now, though anything beyond that was still up to her discretion. It wasn't long before Nick rapped at her door. Opening it, Crista viewed the suave, worldly figure he cut in his white dinner jacket with misgivings.

"Hello," she managed.

He gave her a rakish smile. "You look delightful, Crista," he murmured as he kissed her hand with unsettling grace. "I shall thoroughly enjoy being the envy of Laura's other male guests."

Before she could review her alternatives again, Nick had settled her in his magnificent driving machine and they were off, growling around the hairpin turns and cliff-edged stretches of the south-coast road.

As it turned out, the elegant home where the party was to take place wasn't very far from her hotel. Crowning a hill that looked out over rounded green headlands and a sweeping bay of lapis and turquoise, the sprawling white dwelling had a modern, almost cubist air. Yet it was clearly a part of St. Croix history. Tucked into a right angle of its vaguely L-shaped configuration was the relic of sugar-plantation days Nick had mentioned. Primitively fashioned of rough-cut stone, the semiconical tower of the estate's ancient mill overlooked the deep aquamarine rectangle of an Olympic-size swimming pool.

As Nick parked the car, Crista caught the strains of what might be Brazilian music, a wave of laughter, the clink of glasses and the low murmur of conversation. A bright green-and-yellow parrot flew screeching out of a banana tree when they approached the front door.

The house's interior was gleaming white, airy and whimsical in the extreme. Burnt-orange, overstuffed sofas and chairs were informally arranged on patterned Oriental rugs over terra-cotta flooring. Purple and cream pillows provided additional splashes of color, as did a bewildering array of tropical flowers and greenery. Laura Bettendorf's idiosyncratic taste was further reflected in an extensive collection of Polynesian tribal masks and native Caribbean art. Her furniture was a mix of modern pieces and Danish antiques.

Their hostess greeted them in party pajamas of gold-spangled, semitransparent purple silk. "I'm so glad to meet you, my dear," the slim blonde of indeterminate age told Crista as Nick introduced them. "I understand you're a writer. Come meet Gordon Massey. You'll recall that his latest mystery thriller, *Last Rites For a First Violinist*, is on the bestseller list."

Giving her an encouraging smile, Nick wandered off to speak to some friends. Crista felt somewhat out of her league, chatting with the witty, stylish author and his companion, a lovely part-Irish, part-Creole woman from Montserrat. Luckily, her experience as a reporter who occasionally interviewed well-known people stood her in good stead.

When Nick returned to her side, she found him an amusing and considerate date. Thanks to his attentions and the need to keep up her end in a series of wide-ranging conversations, she didn't have much time to speculate about the evening's outcome. Yet, deep down, she was dreading the moment of truth when she'd have to decide whether or not to ask him to make love to her. Perhaps *let* him would be more appropriate, she thought.

While Crista was mingling with Laura Bettendorf's distinguished guests, Phil was parked below the brow of the hill in his minijeep, trying to decide on a course of action. If he crashed the party, Crista might well refuse to speak to him again. And in one sense, he couldn't blame her. But he was desperate to learn what was going on.

Suddenly an idea suggested itself. Though it wasn't exactly brilliant, it was the only one that came to mind. Checking the amount of cash in his billfold, he got out and clambered up the hillside, taking care to remain hidden from possible observation above.

For a moment he watched the festivities from a thicket of oleanders at the edge of the terrace. Though it looked as if everyone was having a marvelous time, he didn't see Crista. As he'd hoped, uniformed waiters were circulating among the guests, serving drinks from silver trays.

Scrambling around to what he perceived was the entrance, he accosted a slim, dark-haired waiter who spoke with a Puerto Rican accent. "Fifty bucks to wear your jacket and take your place for the rest of the evening, Charlie," he proposed, lightly resting one hand on the man's shoulder.

Startled, the waiter eyed Phil with suspicion. "What for you want to do that, man?" he asked. "This gig don't even pay that much."

Phil hesitated. He decided to tell the truth. "I want to keep an eye on somebody," he confessed. "A girl."

The waiter gave him a sympathetic chuckle. "I get it," he said. "But I could lose my job over this."

"Make it seventy-five." Phil counted out the additional money. "That ought to reimburse you for the risk."

Eyeing the crisp bills, the waiter stretched out his hand for them. Silently he unbuttoned his gray serving jacket.

Phil's Melrose Park relatives would probably have called the whimsically decorated salon a "living room," though it hardly seemed to fit into such a mundane category. Walking in casually, as if he had a perfect right to be there, Phil began to circulate with the waiter's fully laden tray. He had no way of knowing who had ordered what. If something looks familiar, they can grab it, he shrugged to himself as he surveyed the milling partygoers.

He spotted Crista a moment later. She was dancing with Nick in front of open patio doors that faced the terrace and a sky full of stars. As Phil watched, his rival put both arms around her and rested his cheek against her hair. They were moving body to body, separated only by his superbly tailored dinner jacket and trousers, and her flirtatious, strapless dress.

Usually in relatively firm control of his hot Italian temper, Phil saw red. No way was that slimeball of a Caribbean Don Juan going to deflower his girl! Elbowing several guests aside, he barged across the room.

"Cocktail?" he asked rudely, thrusting his precariously poised drinks at the dancing couple.

"Not now, thanks," Nick replied with some asperity.

"How about you, lady?" The question was phrased in Phil's broadest Chicago accent.

Glancing over her shoulder, Crista did a double take. She gasped in horror.

"You!" she exclaimed, her enlarged pupils swallowing up the green of her irises. "I don't believe it! I'm not going to stand for this!"

Peremptorily Phil seized her by the arm as Nick stood there, seemingly rooted to the spot. "You've got no choice in the matter," he declared, pawning off the drinks on an astonished matron and dragging Crista out beside the pool. "You're coming back to the hotel with me. That guy's much too old for you."

A short time earlier, Crista had been wondering if Nick was moving in for the kill. She'd been hovering at the point of asking him to take her home and giving up on the entire escapade, when Phil had appeared. Now the latter's outrageous behavior made her dig in her heels.

"*I*'ll decide who I see and who I don't!" she insisted. "Let go of me!"

A shocked murmur arose from bystanders. They stood frozen in surprise as one of the waiters appeared to make off with a female guest. As Crista struggled to free herself, Nick recovered sufficiently from his astonishment to come to her rescue.

"Hold it right there," Crista's escort warned as he separated them with unexpected force. "This young lady is my date. Just who do you think you are?"

"I happen to be a friend—one who's concerned about her welfare," Phil shot back, assessing his opponent's physical strength. "She's too young and innocent to be keeping company with the likes of you."

Nick's voice took on an ominous tone at the unsavory implication. "And what might that be?" he asked.

Meanwhile Crista's eyes had filled with tears. Despite her profound embarrassment, however, the tears didn't stem from frustration. Instead, she was angrier than she'd ever been in her life.

"*I'*ll decide who I keep company with—and it isn't going to be you!" she snapped. "Get out of here and leave me alone!"

"You heard the young lady," Nick added. "Make yourself scarce before I do something you'll regret."

"Not without Crista." Stubbornly Phil captured her hand.

Taller and more muscular than his rival, he hadn't bargained on Nick's karate expertise. Before he quite realized what was happening to him, he found himself being flipped through the air and landing with a resounding splash in the pool.

Weighted down by street shoes, trousers and his borrowed waiter's jacket, Phil sank to the bottom like a stone. Chlorinated water, which he hated, rushed into his ears and nostrils.

Thrashing wildly, he rose to the surface and climbed out, looking like a cross between a drowned rat and a scarecrow. By now, the entire crowd at the party was buzzing at his plight. As he blinked the water out of his eyes, Phil could see that Crista was red-faced and furious.

"Are you all right?" she asked, her eyes blazing with a mixture of wrath and concern. She hoped he couldn't detect the secret flattery and sympathy she felt.

"Oh, sure... Just fabulous!"

On his way to becoming a nationally known columnist and previously convinced that he had the world by the tail, Phil had never felt so humiliated. What on earth was he doing here on this remote island, chasing after a stubborn and contrary woman?

Feeling sorrier for Phil by the minute, Crista whispered a few words of reassurance to Nick, then fell into step with the man she loved as he plodded back to his minijeep. With each step he took, his shoes made a squishing sound.

Pausing to dump the water out of them, he turned to her. "Are you leaving with me?" he demanded. "Because if not, you're on your own, lady!"

Crista bristled at his fighting words. Her sympathy melted like snow in April. How dare he talk to her that way?

Combatively she rested one hand on her hip. "Nick will look after me, thank you very much!"

Her rejection was an added blow, but he didn't let her see how depressed it made him. "Okay, Little Red Riding Hood," he rasped. "If the wolf turns out to have sharp teeth, don't come running to me for first aid."

Phil! Crista groaned as he took off down the drive, spinning his wheels and scattering gravel in all directions, *you always know just how to pull my chain. I don't want to go through with this and deep in your heart you realize that. I just hope you'll understand later that I did it for us.*

Chapter Nine

Heartsore and inwardly cringing at the curious glances she expected to receive from the other guests, Crista returned to the terrace. She couldn't decide if she was relieved or humiliated at the polite way they avoided her eyes. How in the world was she going to explain to Nick—if he was still willing to listen to anything she had to say.

The extent of his forbearance surprised her.

"Let's get out of here...go somewhere quiet and talk," he suggested, his deeply accented tone a low whisper as he slipped one arm about her waist.

"Yes, I suppose we should," she agreed.

He certainly deserved an explanation. She suspected it wasn't every friend of Bunny Sharpe's he'd met who had a would-be abductor snapping at her heels.

On the other hand, Nick might be more interested in a quick roll in the hay than in talking about Phil. Well, supposedly that was what she wanted, too. She'd expended a great deal of effort and more money than she could afford to get rid of her virginity, and she hadn't managed it yet.

Still, as she thanked Laura Bettendorf for her hospitality and allowed Nick to lead her to his car, Crista wished from the depths of her soul that she could be wherever Phil was at the moment—even if that meant finding herself embroiled in another argument.

The "somewhere quiet" Nick had mentioned turned out to be his low, Bahamas-style bungalow on the island's northeast coast. In contrast to the eclectic chic of the sugar-mill house where the party had been held, the exterior of his home was both traditional and modest. Something about the way it was framed by a low wall and a riot of bougainvillea and banana trees reminded her of a Winslow Homer watercolor. It had a stunning view of the water. From its brick-paved entry court, she could see a cruise ship, extravagantly lit against the sea's blackness as it proceeded to its destination.

Sparsely furnished, the house's interior contained an extensive collection of ultramodern art. It told her little about what to expect from Nick Danzen as a person. Yet its sophistication seemed to fit the man. Clearly an accomplished host, he poured out a bubbly, much-prized vintage of champagne into tulip-shaped glasses and motioned her to join him on the terrace.

"Want to tell me about it?" he said.

The invitation was low-key, clearly designed to be nonthreatening. Settled in a deck chair beside him, overlooking the water, Crista appreciated his sensitivity. But she wasn't sure how to answer him. Should she recite the whole story? Or attempt to dismiss Phil as the kind of maniac who got fixated on some unlucky woman and followed her to the ends of the earth?

If I weren't so much in love with Phil, either Peter or Nick would be the catch of the century, Crista thought. They're both such thoroughly nice men. She realized that most women in her situation would have turned up a pair of gigolos.

Sipping at the dry, effervescent champagne, she decided to tell Nick everything. Though his eyebrows lifted occasionally in amusement or surprise as she spoke, he didn't interrupt the flow of her narrative. Only when she'd finished did he truly react, and then after weighing his words for a moment.

"Do you honestly mean to tell me you've never slept with a man?" he asked in a quiet voice.

"That's right," Crista admitted, feeling like a schoolgirl. "I didn't think it was the right thing to do. I was saving myself for the man I would marry someday."

Nick shook his head. "I didn't know there were any women like you left in the world."

Beneath the irony of his comment, she caught a strong undertone of respect. He didn't think her a fool at all.

"So you're in love with your brash Chicago tough who's also a promising newspaper columnist," Nick observed at last. "What do you propose to do about it? Or maybe I should ask what role you expect *me* to play in all this."

A long pause followed during which Crista shakily considered her options. She hadn't expected such a forthright question, and she wasn't totally prepared to deal with it. Part of her had been holding on to the fiction that even now, Phil might be lurking in the bushes. Her most romantic self still hoped he'd appear to say that he had changed his mind, thus saving her from herself.

It wasn't going to happen. The humiliating plunge into Laura Bettendorf's pool had finally discouraged him. Henceforth, she was strictly on her own. Only she could determine what to do. The moment of truth she'd been dreading had arrived.

If I don't go ahead with this, she tormented herself, Phil and I will drift apart. Ultimately I'll lose him to another woman. And I love him with all my heart.

"I'd like you to make love to me," she told Nick, swallowing to ease the sudden dryness in her throat.

He regarded her without speaking. His calm blue gaze didn't give away his thoughts.

"I know it's asking a lot," she added, trying somehow to fill up the silence. "I've already admitted I'm crazy about someone else. But you're experienced, decent and a real gentleman, Nick. I *like* you, even though I don't know you well. Couldn't that be reason enough?"

"It is for some people," he answered thoughtfully, finishing his champagne. "Why don't we dance a little while I mull over your proposition?"

Arriving back at the hotel complex, Phil changed into dry clothes within the drab confines of his unfinished timeshare apartment. He was in a terrible mood. Not only had he made a complete fool of himself, he'd failed miserably in his objective. Unless he was very much mistaken, Crista was determined to carry out her damned fool scheme. He didn't have a snowball's chance in hell of stopping her; kidnapping was a federal offense.

The thought of another man invading her sweetness nearly drove him out of his head. With a heartfelt oath, he draped his wet things over the naked shower-rod of his minuscule bath. It was too early to stretch out on his lonely mattress. If he did, he'd only lie there awake, racked with painful thoughts.

What he needed was a good stiff drink. A study in controlled fury, he strode across the road and down the broad, winding steps to the hotel's alfresco bar. The usual combo was playing beside the pool, with an emphasis on island rhythms. Turning away from the music and the floodlit blue water that reminded him so piquantly of his folly, he ordered a double Scotch. Morosely sipping it, he tried to think of nothing at all.

Images of Crista kept popping into his head. He imagined her swimming over the reef in her skimpy yellow bikini, her slim, tanned body as graceful as any mermaid's. In his mind's eye, he saw her stalking the streets of Christiansted, furious with him as she plied camera and notebook. Against his will, the images merged and yielded to one of her in the arms of her middle-aged escort, her flirty polka-dot dress unzipped to the waist.

Groaning in anguish, Phil drained his glass. God help him, but he'd been at the point of discussing marriage with her! Only her erratic, willful behavior had prevented him from making such a colossal mistake.

So absorbed was he in his self-induced torture that at first, he didn't notice the buxom, deftly made-up blonde seated just a few barstools away. If he had, he'd have realized in an instant that she'd noticed him.

He was forced to acknowledge her presence when she stood him to a refill. "Thanks," he nodded curtly. "I can use it tonight."

The blonde smiled, undeterred by the brevity of his response. "Hi, I'm Lolly Davison from New York," she said, moving over to sit next to him. "What's your name?"

Deeply angry at Crista, Phil suddenly saw a chance to get back at her. "Phil Catterini, Chicago," he replied, easing the growl out of his voice. "You staying here at the Crescent Beach?"

She didn't need much encouragement. Quickly he extracted the information that she'd come to St. Croix to meet her married boyfriend. Despite lavish promises of a week together in the sun, the boyfriend had bombed out on her. She was all alone.

"He claims he had to stay home with the kids because his wife was rushed to the hospital for an emergency appendectomy," she said philosophically. "I doubt if that's true, don't you? Acute appendicitis isn't all that common these days. I have a feeling she found out about us."

What a refreshing change from Crista, Phil thought, letting the mellow glow induced by the Scotch take hold of his misery and gently nudge it aside. Here's a woman with probably no scruples and few expectations beyond going to bed. He'd known hundreds like her—a few intimately. You could meet one most any night at your neighborhood bar.

"That's too bad," he sympathized, deciding to relax and let her pursue him. "Sounds like your vacation is ruined."

Lolly leaned forward, giving him an unobstructed view down the front of her dress. "Worse things could happen, honey." She shrugged. "I thought as long as he didn't show and that little brunette you've been chasing after has obviously found herself another guy, we could commiserate."

Dancing in Nick's arms at the edge of the terrace, Crista swayed to the lazy trumpet of Dizzy Gillespie, which floated from the outdoor speakers of a first-class stereo. They had drunk more champagne than she was used to and she could feel herself getting a little tight.

To make matters worse, Nick's warm and oh-so-experienced hand was stroking the expanse of bare back exposed by her polka-dot party dress. Just being touched by him that way was making her nervous, though she knew it was supposed to have a calming effect.

He hasn't said yet whether or not he'll make love to me, she thought. All her woman's instincts argued that the answer would be *yes*. First, she guessed, he'd try to trick her into letting down her guard in the hope of making things easier for both of them. All she could think of was her strong desire to be dancing in Phil's arms instead.

"Why don't we take off our shoes," Nick suggested as a slow number came to an end. "There's something incredibly sensuous about dancing barefoot."

Not at all sure she *wanted* to be "incredibly sensuous," Crista complied. She was grateful for the momentary release from intimate contact with Nick's dangerous masculinity as she bent over to unfasten her sandals.

Why can't I just yield up my maidenhood like swallowing a dose of bitter-tasting medicine and get it over with? she asked herself. But apparently it was not to be. Nick seemed determined to initiate her with subtlety and finesse—make her first experience with sex a romantic and memorable one. From an objective point of view, she appreciated his consideration. It was just so hard to remain objective when every neuron in her body wanted to fire her in the direction of another man.

Nick's compact-disc player was set on Repeat and the first torchy selection came on again. As he took her back into his arms, he kissed her hair, her neck, the bare curve of her shoulder.

"You have the most beautiful skin, Crista O'Malley," he whispered, sending chills of apprehension down her spine. "Completely satiny and flawless. I'd like to see all of it, gleaming like alabaster in the moonlight. What would you say to a nice, relaxing soak in my hot tub?"

"Your... *hot tub*?" Crista breathed. "I didn't see..."

He gave her a wry smile. "That's because it's in my bedroom and we haven't been there yet. Don't worry.... We won't have to give up the lovely fresh air of the terrace. My sliding glass doors open to the view."

Back at the hotel, Phil continued to nurse his grudge against Crista as he basked in Lolly's attention. Her flirtatious chatter was like balm to his ego. Throwing discretion to the breeze that rustled in the coconut palms, he encouraged her—even though he realized that in the long run she wasn't for him.

Funny, he thought. She's a lot like Irene, if not quite as intelligent. They're the same physical type: the kind of woman I used to go for like a shot. Had Crista somehow put a spell on him, forcing him to compare busty, accommodating blondes unfavorably with petite, dark-haired women most notable for their stubbornness? It wouldn't have surprised him in the least.

With seduction gleaming in her eyes, Lolly asked Phil to dance. Immediately the leader of the little combo noted their involvement. His amiable face creasing in a knowing smile, he switched over to a slower, more romantic number.

Perhaps moved by the throb of steel drums and guitars, perhaps by the tang of Phil's after-shave, Lolly snuggled up to him, playfully nibbling at his earlobe. Her large bosom pressed suggestively against his chest.

"I never dated a newspaperman before," she said in her husky voice. "I'll bet you're good with words, honey. You probably know how to say lots of sexy, mind-blowing stuff."

At Nick's beachfront bungalow, Crista stood petrified in the master bath, wrapped in an oversize towel. Nick had suggested she disrobe in privacy after she'd flatly refused to do so in front of him. As she'd closeted herself in the bath, she'd heard him uncork a second bottle of champagne. Now he was waiting for her—already comfortably naked—in his bubbling, sky-blue tub.

I'm not sure I can go through with this, she told herself, staring at her anguished face in the mirror. Even getting into the water with him minus my suit goes against my deepest, most ingrained beliefs. She felt like Susannah about to be put on display before the elders. Her natural modesty seemed to rise up like a shield.

If I don't snatch the opportunity while it's mine, I'll find myself back at square one with Phil, she reminded herself unsteadily. And I don't believe I could bear that, either. Something has to give between us.

Still wrapped in her towel, she stepped timidly out into Nick's airy, neutral-toned bedroom, taking care not to glance at his king-size bed. To her dismay, she saw there were mirrors on the ceiling. Her steps became more reluctant as she advanced toward the man from whom she'd requested such a bizarre and intimate favor.

Nick was waist-deep in gurgling bubbles. He held his champagne glass in his hand. "C'mon in," he coaxed with a grin. "The water's fine. If you want me to, I'll shut my eyes."

Crista's hand hesitated at the corner of the towel, which she'd stuffed tightly between her breasts. *No,* she realized. *I can't do this.* In that split-second flash of blinding clarity, she knew she couldn't possibly accept his invitation. Maybe before Phil, she could have forced herself to make love to Nick simply to get rid of her virginity; but she doubted it. Now it would be like a form of self-immolation.

"You've been awfully sweet and accommodating, but I can't go through with this," she declared, keeping her gaze above the level of his chin. "I love Phil, and I'm stuck with being faithful to him even if that ruins my chances. Would it be too much of an inconvenience for you to get dressed and take me back to my hotel?"

At the Crescent Beach, Lolly was leading Phil up the stairs toward her room. "What you need is a little affection, honey," she told him, her arm about his waist. "Give me half a chance and I can make you forget that skinny little dark-haired girl."

Maybe, he thought, as she opened the door and led him into a room identical to Crista's, though I doubt it. At least I won't have to sleep on that damn mattress tonight. He didn't want to think about the likelihood that he wouldn't be able to perform to Lolly's satisfaction. He was much too tired and out of sorts, and he'd had too much alcohol.

Hell, he swore silently, you might as well face it. The truth is, she isn't Crista. But if you let that bother you, you're even crazier than you thought.

No sooner had Phil disappeared inside Lolly's room than Nick and Crista arrived back at the hotel. He handed her out of the Porsche in front of the open-air lobby.

"Good night and thank you," she whispered shyly, giving him a reserved peck on the cheek. "I have a lot to thank you for, not the least of which has been your forbearance."

Nick's eyes twinkled with ironic humor. "It was my pleasure," he answered. "It's certainly been an experience knowing you. I wonder if that good-looking party crasher of yours realizes how lucky he is."

* * *

In Lolly's room, Phil sat on the edge of her bed and switched on the television as she disappeared into the bathroom to "slip into something more comfortable." He hadn't had access to a set since leaving Chicago and he wondered how the Black Hawks were doing. Maybe there'd be some late sports news.

He was flabbergasted a minute or two later when Lolly returned without a stitch.

"Hi there, Phil, baby," she teased, her large breasts jiggling as she approached. "Aren't you a teeny bit overdressed?"

Without question, she was a sexy sight. Yet to Phil's amazement, he didn't feel anything but alarm at her nakedness. What if Crista finds out? he asked himself. She'll never speak to me again if I turn her down and then take a stranger to bed.

Even more astonishing was the fact that he didn't feel the slightest bit titillated by such a lush example of feminine pulchritude. But the truth was, Crista was the only woman he really wanted.

"Sorry," he muttered, brushing past the bewildered Lolly as he headed out the door. "I've got to see a phone book about an address...."

As Nick drove off, Crista was asking for Phil's room number at the front desk. Her heart sank when the clerk told her he wasn't registered. How on earth was she going to find him? He could be anywhere on the island—maybe even at the airport.

Noting her distress, the night manager came over and spoke to her in a low tone. "You looking for Mr. Philip Catterini, miss?" he inquired.

"Yes, it's very urgent," she said.

For a moment the manager hesitated. Then, "He's staying at the condos across the road...number 204 in the unfinished section," he informed her. "Please don't tell anyone."

So *that*'s the kind of deal Phil worked to hang around and maintain his surveillance of me at all hours, she thought with grudging admiration as she crossed the narrow ribbon of blacktop that separated the condos from the hotel. I have to hand it to him. I wonder what he's going to say when I show up at his door. Hopefully he won't still be angry at the dunking he received.

As she started up the stairs to his room, Phil strode into the lobby and began pawing through the telephone book. He'd managed to pry Nick Danzen's name from Crista before she'd clammed up, fearing he would follow her. Now, provided he could find the man's address, he had every intention of kidnapping her for both their sakes. So what if she had him arrested afterward?

The unfinished section of condos was murky with shadows, still littered here and there with building materials. Crista had to watch her step. Pounding on the door the night manager had indicated, she didn't get a response. At last she had to concede that Phil probably wasn't inside.

Dejectedly she started back across the road near the tennis courts. What now? she asked herself. Have I lost him? Appearing from nowhere, a pair of headlights aimed straight for her. Transfixed by their glare and the tears that were welling up in her eyes, she was almost run over by Phil's minijeep.

In the nick of time he screeched to a halt. "Get in!" he barked furiously, leaning across the passenger seat to open the door.

Her eyes wide, Crista complied without a word. The jeep's tires squealed again as he took off down the coast road, seemingly bent on venting his wrath in a burst of reckless driving. She didn't dare remonstrate.

A few minutes later he made a sharp left turn onto a deserted spit of land that protruded into Grapetree Bay. Earlier, one of the shuttle drivers had referred to it as "lovers' lane." By now the moon was high. Its silver hem trailed across the water, illuminating their faces as they lurched to a halt and Phil cut the Jeep's engine.

She could feel him forcing down his ire into some emotional bastion deep within himself. Gradually his breath came more easily and his hands no longer gripped the wheel. "Want to tell me what happened?" he asked after the silence between them had stretched to the breaking point.

"Nothing," Crista admitted in a small voice.

"You mean..."

"I couldn't go through with it. I made him bring me back to the hotel."

Relief surged through Phil like a tidal wave. He felt as if he'd just been handed the most magnificent present.

"Neither could I, sweetheart," he murmured, not stopping to explain about Lolly as he crushed Crista in his arms. "We're having one hell of a vacation apart, aren't we? What do you say we spend the rest of our time on St. Croix together?"

Chapter Ten

It was as if a dam had broken. The reservoir of her separateness spilling over, Crista burrowed against the oh-so-comforting wall of his chest. Phil hadn't gone. He didn't hate her. There was still a chance for them. She wanted to become so deeply enmeshed with him that no one could ever separate them.

"Oh, Phil," she babbled, not certain if she was making any sense. "The first clerk told me you weren't staying at the hotel. I didn't know how to find you, to apologize for what happened. I thought maybe you'd be at the airport, changing your ticket home...."

"Hush, sweetheart. Don't cry. You know I'd never leave you down here all by yourself."

Tenderly Phil stroked her hair, luxuriating in its silky texture and subtle perfume. Condemned to the depths of misery only a few minutes before, now he felt like he owned the world. So what if they were back at the same old impasse? They'd find some way to handle it.

For her part, Crista sensed a feeling of expectancy in the way they held each other. It was as if one or more of the stumbling blocks that had impeded a more profound relationship between them had suddenly been removed. She wasn't sure exactly *what* had happened—just that she was deliriously happy not to be at odds with him. She'd take any risk, do whatever was necessary, to safeguard such a blissful state.

"Sure you're not angry?" she whispered.

He shook his head. "I'm the one who should be apologizing to you for trying to drag you away from that party," he said, not bothering to admit that he'd been on the verge of embarrassing her again. "I just couldn't help it. I lost it when I saw you in Nick Danzen's arms."

Crista gave a little quivering sigh. "I realize now I never could have gone through with it," she admitted. "No matter how outrageously you behaved. Promise me you won't be upset if I tell you why."

A feeling of fatalism washed over him. "Go ahead...tell me," he answered, the gentle rasp of his voice giving her all the reassurance she needed.

"Because I wanted it to be you."

"Oh, baby..." With a groan, he tightened his embrace, kissing her forehead, her cheek, the tender spot just behind her ear.

For the first time, he realized just what his refusal had cost her. I don't know what we're going to do about this, he told her silently, sheltering her in his arms. Something tells me we're on the brink of a solution. It's just that I'm too exhausted, too emotionally wrung out from the evening's misadventures to come up with one tonight.

"Sweetheart," he asked her, "would you be willing to let things settle for a few days? Just see what happens? Ultimately, of course, we'll have to talk."

"Yes," Crista answered without hesitation. She didn't dare put everything she was feeling just then into words. "About tonight..."

Lightly Phil kissed the tip of her nose. "I'm too beat and I've had too much to drink to be a threat to anyone," he admitted. "But I want to sleep with you...hold you in my arms in the same bed. Would you consider letting me share your room?"

The smile that curved her lips would have done credit to an angel. "I was just going to ask you the same question," she said.

He shook his head. "Hell, baby, you don't know what you'd have been letting yourself in for. You wouldn't want to share the digs *I've* been operating from."

Reluctantly easing her off his lap, Phil started up the minijeep and drove to the condo to pick up his bags. Crista stared at the inadequate mattress someone had placed directly on the carpeting. A tangle of sheets bore mute testimony to several restless nights.

A few minutes later they were unlocking the door to her room. Phil threw his duffel down beside the dresser and looked around. Like Crista's Chicago apartment, the room was neat. It seemed odd but incredibly right that their things should be contained in the same space.

Crista watched him as if she were making a similar discovery. Giving her a brief, hard kiss, he stretched out on the tropical-print coverlet. "You first in the shower, babycakes," he said with an enormous yawn. "I need a few minutes to get reacquainted with a real bed."

Crista turned on the shower with a sigh of contentment. Stepping beneath the spray, she closed her eyes and let the water stream over her body. *I can hardly believe it*, she thought, hugging herself. *But we're here, in the same room together. Me and Phil Catterini—the tough, hand-*

some and immensely talented columnist who once seemed so unapproachable. Me and Phil Catterini—the man I love.

She knew he wouldn't make love to her that night and she didn't mind. They were both tired, worse from the wear of too much emotional upheaval. Both had drunk too much alcohol. But there was hope. Out at "lovers' lane" he'd proposed they spend the rest of the week together. Anything could happen in the next few days!

While she sudsed and rinsed, Phil pulled back the spread and dozed. The pillow slips were lightly scented with her perfume and he inhaled it with pleasure. He hadn't felt so relaxed, so comfortable, in weeks.

His eyes opened when she came out of the bath with damp hair and rosy cheeks. She was wearing a modest, flower-sprigged nightdress of cotton lawn that looked as if it had been chosen by her grandmother. Her soft mouth and dark lashes were innocent of makeup.

Was it possible he'd once classified her as "almost pretty"? To Phil at that moment, Crista was the most beautiful woman in the world. Suddenly not trusting himself despite his weariness, he got to his feet.

"I won't be long," he said, heading into the bathroom.

She was still awake when he came out clad only in a fresh pair of boxer shorts and got into bed. Is this really us? he asked himself as he reached over and turned out the light. What's going to happen tomorrow, when we've had some sleep?

The wisest part of him refused to search for an answer. As instinctively as if they'd shared the same bed for years, he reached for her in the dark. Sighing, she snuggled against him. His lips found hers and they kissed once, twice, holding each other tightly as they acknowledged the stirring of a passion that wouldn't long be denied.

A moment later, they rearranged themselves with her head pillowed in the curve of his shoulder. We're going to want each other again tomorrow, Crista thought as wakefulness blurred into sleep. And I'm not sure what we're going to do about that. The only thing I know with any certainty is that I want to spend the rest of my life with him.

When she awoke the next morning, Phil was gone. She experienced a momentary stab of panic before she realized the shower was running again. Was he a cleanliness freak? she wondered. Or was it cold water this time? She was willing to bet money the latter guess was right, if the dream she'd had just before awakening was any indication of how he felt.

There was a long silence after the water was shut off. Finally Phil emerged fully dressed in shorts and a Ski Bum T-shirt he'd apparently picked up in Vail. His hair was clinging in damp points to his forehead.

"Your turn," he said awkwardly, unable to take his eyes off the slender but voluptuous sight she made as she threw back the top sheet and flung her bare legs over the side of the bed. "If you hurry, I might be persuaded to buy breakfast for us both."

Crista wasn't fooled by his casual tone. She guessed he was eager to get her out of the room before anything could happen between them. Okay by me, she thought. Little Miss Fix-It that I am, I'm through trying to manipulate things. Instead, I'll put my trust in fate. Go with the flow and see what happens. If he cares for me half as much as I do for him, things will work out for the best.

Needing only a quick sponge bath, a session with her toothbrush and a dash of lipstick, she was dressed and ready in just a few minutes. "What's on the agenda for today?" she asked as she stood before the mirror vigorously applying a hairbrush to her smooth, mahogany-lit page boy.

Phil had never known a woman so unself-conscious, so unaffected, so totally herself. Every new facet of Crista O'Malley was a delicious revelation.

"I saw something about speedboat races on the activity board in the lobby," he answered. "That might be fun. I understand the hotel provides everything."

The Crescent Beach's breakfast buffet was set up around the little bar where Crista had met Peter Vandervelt on the night of her arrival and where Phil had been approached by Lolly just a few hours before. Piles of fresh fruit, muffins, bacon and scrambled eggs beckoned. A smiling girl in a sarong was extracting fresh orange juice with the aid of an electric juicer. The just-ground coffee smelled like heaven in a cup.

Phil and Crista were drinking their juice at one of the umbrella-topped tables when a hotel employee approached. With a grin, the man handed her a showy bouquet of tropical flowers. "Florist leave this for you at the front desk, miss," he said.

The bouquet was decorated with a huge pink ribbon. Taken aback, Crista buried her face among its fragrant petals while Phil tipped the bearer.

"Who's it from?" he asked with a frown as she braced herself. "I think I saw an envelope."

As Crista feared, the bouquet was from Nick. Scanning the few lines her erstwhile escort had penned, she admitted as much.

"Sure nothing happened last night?" Phil asked, trying to make the query sound like a joke.

Fortunately the card exonerated her. "Thanks for one of the finest evenings I almost had," Nick had written.

"Good luck with your boyfriend. Stop and see me at the store if you have a chance."

Relieved, Phil realized he was ravenously hungry. Diving into his scrambled eggs and buttering a croissant, he didn't see Lolly Davison approach their table until it was too late.

A moment later, the remainder of Phil's orange juice was dumped unceremoniously in his lap. The hand responsible had long, red fingernails.

"*That*'s for leaving me in the lurch, you jerk!" Lolly hissed, giving him a venomous look. "If you were the only man on this island, I'd choose to spend my vacation alone!"

This time it was Crista's turn to ask a few pointed questions. She didn't pass up the opportunity as Phil mopped up the spill. But they were tongue-in-cheek and she laughed outright when he told her the truth. Suddenly he, too, could see the humor in the situation.

"I hope this teaches you a lesson," she teased. "You're much better off with me, despite my willful ways and dreadful Irish temper. At least I don't pour my breakfast in your lap!"

Phil gave her hand an affectionate squeeze. "I don't know which is worse," he countered, merriment dancing in his hazel eyes. "Being thrown, fully clothed, into an overly chlorinated pool or having your private parts marinated in orange juice. With you, I've learned I'd better be prepared for anything."

After returning to her room and changing into their swimsuits, Phil and Crista signed up for the speedboat race organized by the resort's preppy, athletic-looking activities director. Right at home behind the wheel of any powerful machine, Phil happily assumed the role of captain and relegated Crista to the position of first mate. Though a firm proponent of equal rights for women, she didn't mind in the least. After his terrible experience snorkeling over the reef, she was glad to see him have some fun.

Revving up at the starting line, they exchanged a grin. We're a team, Crista exulted. Us against them. The feeling was better than any prize.

The race—from the hotel pier out to the reef and back again—took only a few hectic minutes. Splashed by salt spray with his unruly hair whipping in the breeze, Phil didn't seem to feel any seasickness. His firmly hewn features were alight with pleasure.

God, but he's gorgeous, Crista thought, letting her gaze rest on his hair-roughened chest and muscular biceps as they lunged forward, bouncing on the surface of the water as if it were plywood. Even in that situation, with its bone-jarring excitement, every fiber of her being was aching to know Phil's body even more intimately than her own.

To both their surprise, they finished in second place. The reward was a bottle of champagne. To celebrate, they took a lazy swim in the shallow waters of the bay, followed by a hotly competitive set of tennis. Phil emerged victorious by a single game, forcing Crista to pay for the piña coladas they'd wagered for.

Except for the absence of sex and the way both of them avoided any mention of future hopes and dreams, it was like being on the perfect honeymoon.

"You know what?" Crista asked as they sunned themselves lazily beside the pool. "I think last night is catching up with me. I could use a nap."

For a second, something that looked precariously like lust glittered in Phil's eyes. Just as quickly, it was hidden. There was no telling what might happen if he agreed to join her, now that they were sharing the same room.

"Sounds like a waste of perfectly good vacation time to me," he answered, firmly vetoing her idea as he pulled her to her feet. "Let's change our clothes and go shopping instead. It's not every day you get to spend money in a free port."

When a man suggests a shopping trip, Crista thought as they went up to her room to change, you know he has an ulterior motive. However, she'd promised herself she wouldn't cause problems. By now she was ready for another shower to remove the film of saltwater crystals that had accumulated on her skin. Closeting herself in the bathroom, she took off her suit and got into the shower stall. She'd just managed to get herself thoroughly wet when the water slowed to a trickle, then stopped altogether.

"Hey!" she yelled. "Something's wrong with the water! There *isn't* any!"

Though Phil jumped up from his chair on the balcony at the sound of her voice, he couldn't make out what she was saying. Aware only of a definite note of distress, he burst into the bathroom to find her stepping out of the shower enclosure. She was dripping wet and a small towel barely covered her.

For a moment they simply stared at each other. Like those of a starving man, Phil's eyes devoured the sight of the scant towel clinging to her perfect breasts, slender waist and curving hips. Her thighs were shapely and firm; he could imagine them gripping him in the throes of passion.

She was so beautiful it hurt. He wanted to shelter and protect her even as he imagined stripping off all his clothes and plunging deep into her body. Was this what love was all about?

In a sudden spasm of shyness, Crista clutched the towel tightly to her. But as a defensive gesture it was wasted.

Gently Phil took another towel and patted her shoulders and legs dry in what seemed like slow motion. Exquisite, rapier-sharp thrusts of ecstasy pierced the deepest recesses of her being. She thought she would pass out from the delight of having him touch her that way.

Groaning at her loveliness, Phil eased her covering down and dried beneath her breasts. The physical desire he'd been fighting to control from the moment they'd first kissed had thundered over him like an avalanche. Before he'd even realized what he was doing, he was dropping the towel and sweeping her up into his arms.

It was happening at last. Crista nuzzled his neck with a mouth that was eager for more, much more of him. She wanted to take everything he had to give while she burned to ashes on the altar of his need.

"Oh, Phil," she breathed, her fingers digging into his shoulders. "I want you so much."

Her skin was like velvet, the texture of her flesh unbelievably delectable as he carried her to the bed. Their lips met and parted, their tongues explored, and suddenly it was as if they were one person, merging, blending, sinking into a vortex of passion so deep there could be no escape.

Phil's hands on her breasts excited Crista to a fever pitch of desire and anticipation. She cried aloud at the unbearable sweetness of it when he knelt to put his mouth where his hands had been. More vigorously than she'd imagined could be pleasurable he sucked on one hardened nipple, tugging at it as if he could draw the nectar of her essence into himself. With his thumb and forefinger, he kneaded her other peak to taut submission, then laved it with his tongue.

The message of urgency he aroused transmitted itself like lightning to the deep tunnel of Crista's womanhood, causing her to strain and ache for his presence there. Just one touch from him in that place, she thought, and I'll go off like a Roman candle.

Moments later he was atop her, his lower body with its engorged readiness pressing against hers.

"Yes, oh yes..." she pleaded, tangling her fingers in the unruly thicket of his hair. "Take me, I want you to. Please, darling... let me feel you inside me."

With a muffled sound that was like an oath, Phil dragged them both to a sitting position. She was so delicate, so fragile despite her rounded womanliness. He felt like a rake, an unscrupulous Lothario when he saw the trust and generosity shining in her eyes.

"Crista..." he began, his voice husky with a mixture of need and anguish. "You're so lovely. And I want you—more than I've ever wanted a woman. But I'd never forgive myself...."

He was going to turn her down again. Overcome with panic, she wound her arms about his neck. "Phil, *please!*" she begged. "Don't refuse me. I love you so much!"

The words were out before she could stop them. When the truth of them hit home, she flushed in humiliation, burying her face against his shoulder.

For a moment Phil simply held her in his arms. He didn't answer. He was stunned, more stunned than she could possibly guess. I don't deserve to be loved by someone like you, he thought, suddenly seeing things in what he considered their true perspective. At the same time, he was even more amazed by the strong suspicion that he felt exactly as she did.

"Ah, sweetheart," he whispered. "Come, put on your robe. We have to talk about this."

Wrapped in a thin cotton duster with her hair still damp from her abortive shower, Crista faced him forlornly from the edge of the bed. Phil sat across from her in a rattan chair. He had captured both her hands in his. As he looked at her, he felt as if he were stepping off the edge of a cliff, throwing himself into shark-infested waters. But there was no help for it. Though he might not be cut out for the domestic scene, he couldn't live without this moral, frustratingly stubborn and thoroughly delicious woman another twenty-four hours.

Yet he knew he could never allow her to violate her principles for his sake.

When he didn't speak immediately, tears welled up in her eyes. "Forget what I said," she whispered. "We can just be friends. I don't want to lose you."

"Oh, baby..." With a rueful shake of his head, Phil tightened his grip. "I think I feel the same way about you," he confessed.

For the space of a heartbeat Crista thought she was imagining things. Then, "You do?" she asked in amazement.

He nodded, distractedly kissing her fingertips. "The question is, what are we going to do about it?"

"What do *you* want to do about it?" she asked.

Phil hovered on the brink, torn between his need for her and all the prejudices against conjugal bliss he'd nourished for so long. But it wasn't any contest. The die had been cast and he couldn't do without her any longer.

"I think we have to get married," he said slowly. "Right now... *Today* if possible... Before we do something we'll regret."

Crista nearly succumbed to a case of vertigo. Had she really heard what she thought he'd said? She was too flabbergasted to answer him.

"So," he prodded, impatient as always, now that his mind was made up. "Will you marry me? The territorial court will be open for a couple of hours yet."

Phil's proposal was reminiscent of his previous back-handed invitations. Several minutes passed before he could convince Crista he was serious. When he finally did, she admitted she was willing.

"Of course, I'll marry you—if that's what you really want," she replied. "But I'm not sure we should rush ahead the way you're suggesting. There's bound to be a waiting period. And anyway, I've always wanted a formal wedding with a white gown and veil. What will Gran say if we elope?"

What will my family say? he asked himself silently. It was a long-standing Catterini tradition to be married in church. He knew Grandpa Santo and Great-Aunt Rosa would disapprove of anything else.

Yet the more Crista protested, the more determined he was not to take *no* for an answer. "We can do the whole thing over again when we get home if it means that much to you," he promised. "Hurry up and get dressed."

It's what I want, Crista thought dazedly as she put on her laciest underwear and went to the closet for the two-year-old white wool suit she'd brought along to accentuate her winter tan on the return trip. Even if it isn't happening the way I've always pictured it. Do I dare snatch the opportunity, now that it has fallen so unexpectedly into my hands?

Madly in love with Phil, she was afraid he'd wake up later and regret his spur-of-the-moment proposal. In just three days' time, they would be flying back to Chicago and the workaday world. By going along with what he wanted now, was she making a big mistake? Her heart skipping a beat, she decided to take a chance.

Crista knew that even in what passed for January on St. Croix, her suit might prove a bit too warm to be comfortable. But it was the closest thing to a wedding outfit she possessed. Slipping into it, she brushed her hair and applied fresh makeup with shaking fingers. My kingdom for a hat, she thought, stifling the urge to manic laughter that rose in her throat.

As they headed into town, Crista's practical, down-to-earth side was praying there'd be a waiting period. Her romantic and utterly sensual self was terrified they'd have to wait.

In Christiansted they parked beside the harbor and walked the few short blocks to the offices of the territorial court, which were housed in a yellow-and-white Danish colonial building with dark green shutters. Still feeling as if the entire chain of events she'd lived through in the past few days might be a figment of her imagination, Crista almost had to run to keep up with Phil's quick, lengthy strides.

When they applied for the license, they learned there was indeed a waiting period—eight days, to be exact. "How do you go about getting it waived?" Phil asked with his typical newspaperman's I-can-make-anything-happen brand of impatience.

"I'm afraid you'd have to see a judge about that, sir," the clerk replied.

Taking Crista by the hand, Phil headed upstairs to the judge's chambers. Though the secretary to the family-court judge listened patiently to his explanation of what he wanted, she refused to disturb her boss with his request.

"This is an emergency," Phil insisted, leaning with both hands on her desk.

Involuntarily the young woman glanced at Crista's flat stomach. No baby about to be born, no emergency, Crista could almost hear her thinking.

Just as she was about to refuse Phil again, the judge herself suddenly appeared with a sheaf of documents. Before the secretary could stop him, Phil importuned the judge with his plea. She ushered them into her private office.

At first the dignified woman was severe as she reminded them that the waiting period had been instituted for a reason. "Exactly what is the nature of this emergency?" she asked.

Without mincing words, Phil explained their situation. "It's a matter of principle," he concluded. "I can't trust myself not to take advantage of my fiancée unless we're married immediately. And I don't want her ethics violated at the last moment."

A smile hovered about the judge's mouth at the old-fashioned sentiment. "I thought I'd heard every excuse for a waiver, but this is a new one on me," she admitted. "And I agree—preserving virginity unto marriage is a laudable intent. I'll make you a bargain. Buy your young lady a wedding ring and be back here by four-thirty. If you both still want to proceed, I'll marry you myself."

Chapter Eleven

As they stepped out of the courthouse into the strong afternoon sunlight, Phil had a stunned look on his face. He'd actually talked the judge into it! Well, hadn't he expected to?

"Umm... Where do you suppose we ought to look for a ring?" he asked Crista.

As they both knew, Christiansted was full of jewelry shops. But they didn't have much time if they were going to make it back by four-thirty. The question was, where to start?

Embarrassed, Crista had no idea how much Phil wanted to spend. Yet, despite everything that had transpired, she was still friends with Nick.

"What about Nick Danzen's place?" she suggested tentatively. "At least he'd quote us a fair price."

Phil bristled at the thought of patronizing Nick's shop. In his mind, memories of the previous night's humiliating episode were still excruciatingly clear. He was also more than a little upset over what could have occurred if Crista hadn't backed out at the last moment.

Then he mellowed. She was marrying him, after all, not Nick. And the note that had accompanied the older man's flowers that morning had wished her "luck with her boyfriend." There was nothing to be jealous about.

"Sure, why not?" he replied.

Nick was clearly astonished when they walked into his shop together. But he had an even bigger surprise in store. Crista barely managed to get out a "Thank you for the flowers," before Phil pounced on him with a businesslike request.

"We need a wedding and engagement set and we're in something of a hurry," Phil said, rapidly scanning the jewelry cases. "Crista tells me you specialize in emeralds. I hope you take credit cards."

The engagement ring they chose was a small but perfect square-cut emerald, set in platinum and flanked by sparkling baguette diamonds. There was a matching wedding ring. *I could never have afforded anything like this on my crime reporter's salary,* Phil thought. *Now that I'm a man with an excellent position and even better prospects, I suppose it's only fitting that I take a wife.*

Slipping the engagement ring on Crista's finger, he realized it matched the color of her eyes. His brave soliloquy notwithstanding, he had a sinking feeling in the pit of his stomach. In his book, marriage was forever. But though he'd been engaged many times, he'd never actually expected to tie the knot. Now—in less time than he wanted to think about—he'd be a husband.

Even as his courage faltered, he felt a tremendous upsurge of pride that such a delicate, desirable woman—one who'd never given herself to another man—would soon promise to cleave only unto him. Pride vanquishing reluctance, he put one arm around her. Somehow they'd work things out, have the kind of life they both wanted.

This is actually happening, Crista thought, barely able to convince herself of the reality of it. Phil's going to be mine to love and cherish for a lifetime. He'll be the father of my children, the man I sleep with every night. She had to refrain from pinching herself.

"If you'll allow me," Nick murmured, his ironic smile like a benediction when their transaction had been completed, "I'd like to give you two a wedding present—the use of my house for your wedding night. It wouldn't be very romantic just to go back to your hotel."

Phil blinked at the unexpected offer.

"Oh, but we couldn't put you out!" Crista protested.

"You wouldn't be doing that," Nick replied. "The key's under the mat and there are steaks and champagne in the refrigerator. My twice-weekly maid even changed the linen this morning. As for me, I'm taking the seaplane to St. Thomas tonight. I plan to stay over with a friend."

When they returned to the office of the family-court judge, she was straightening her desk and stuffing some papers in her briefcase preparatory to leaving. "Ah," she greeted them with pleasure. "So you came back. I was hoping you would."

Summoning her secretary and a bailiff to act as witnesses, she donned her official robe again. "Ready?" she asked, as Phil and Crista nervously faced her.

They looked at each other, green eyes losing themselves in hazel ones. The future was suddenly resplendent with possibilities. "Yes," they said, almost in unison.

Mercifully the formalities were brief. Though Crista's voice rang out calm and clear as she repeated her vows, Phil's was slightly hoarse and emotional. His hands were shaking as he slipped the wedding band on her finger. Though by now he was convinced that having Crista for his wife was what he wanted more than anything in the world, his sensing, feeling self had undergone a tremendous workout. He realized he couldn't have stood up to the strain of a more elaborate ceremony.

Almost before they knew it, the fateful words had been spoken. It was time for the nuptial kiss. Awed by what had happened, Phil brushed Crista's mouth gently with his own. His heart felt as if it would expand in his chest at the sight of the tears that shone in her eyes.

Moments later the judge was offering her congratulations. "I trust you'll prove me right for having waived the requirements," she declared, beaming at them. "Have a wonderful life."

At that point they'd been engaged for barely two-and-a-half hours. Crista had worn her emerald exactly twenty-eight minutes.

Back out on the street they were forced to duck into a series of covered walkways to avoid a sudden rain shower that slanted through the sun-spangled afternoon. "Where to?" Phil asked as they paused to look at each other.

Suddenly they were laughing and hugging each other, running between the raindrops.

On their way back to the hotel to pick up a change of clothing, Crista and Phil couldn't keep their hands off each other. Pulling her tightly into the curve of his arm, he nuzzled her mouth again and again, even as he tried to watch the road. She was his now. There'd be no more holding back, no thorny ethical problems to face.

Simultaneously he realized the frustration they'd endured had imparted perverse pleasures of its own. Just a taste of that waiting might serve as an aphrodisiac, lending added spice to their banquet now that they were at the brink of fulfillment.

There was also Crista's virginity to think about. You need to take it slow, he counseled himself. She's never done any of the things we're about to do together.

He would make it good for her, he promised himself; give her as much time as she needed to reach the heights. Afterward, they'd explore the age-old mysteries that would be fresh for him, too, with Crista in his arms. Resolutely he pushed down the burgeoning need in his groin that, even now, was struggling to take command of him, bidding to rule his every gesture.

Beneath the thin lace barrier of her bra, Crista's nipples stood erect and ready for his mouth. The familiar, savagely delicious ache he'd taught her suffused her body. Spreading like wildfire, it seared every cell, lit the fuse of every nerve-ending, even as it focused in a fierce eagerness between her legs.

They were both tingling, mindless of anything but the reality of their mutual need by the time they reached the hotel. The minute they entered her room, Crista pleaded with Phil to take her to bed.

Lovingly he refused.

"Why not?" she protested as he began to gather up their things for transport to the bungalow where they planned to spend the night. "I'm your wife now. And I feel like a fully ignited rocket ship that can't get off the launching pad."

Phil gathered her against him, inviting her awareness of the hard, pulsing masculinity that had stiffened at the thought of union with her.

"That's how I feel, too," he told her. "But we don't want our lovemaking to be like a trip through a fast-food restaurant, sweetheart. Your first time...and our first time together... should be more like a gourmet meal, savored in the best possible surroundings. I want us to settle in for the night before we get started, so we can linger over every bite."

Any further complaint she might have wanted to lodge was smothered by a kiss. "Trust me," he urged, tilting her chin so that it was on a level with his. "We'll make love all night long if that's what you want."

Crista found it strange to be walking into Nick's house with Phil—unlocking the same door Nick had held open for her. She wrestled with a sense of déjà vu as she took in Nick's modern furniture and art collection, the expensive stereo that looked as if it belonged in the cockpit of an airplane. Everything appeared as it had the night before. Yet, since she'd last seen these things, her world had shifted on its axis. Life had rearranged itself in a new and blissful configuration.

Despite any meaning the place might have for him, Phil quickly took charge of the situation. Loading a warmly sensuous CD on the stereo and pressing the Repeat button, he carried their things into the master bedroom. Confidently he filled the hot tub and opened the sliding glass doors to the terrace. "After last night, do you want more champagne?" he asked.

Still wearing the trim wool suit she'd been married in, Crista considered. "I guess a little hair of the dog that bit me wouldn't hurt," she said. "We ought to toast our vows."

"I think so, too." Phil disappeared into the kitchen to retrieve a chilled bottle and two glasses.

As she waited for him, Crista suddenly began to get cold feet. For the first time, she wondered if she was equal to the situation. What am I supposed to do? she wondered. Put on a peignoir and act sexy? In point of fact, all she had was a nightgown, and it wasn't the sort she'd have chosen for her honeymoon. Despite her many requests that Phil dispatch her virginity without delay, she began to worry about how things would turn out. Thanks to her inexperience, there wasn't any guarantee that she could satisfy him.

If she expected a barrage of demands, Phil eased her mind when he came back into the room. Ceremoniously popping the cork from a magnum of brut, he did the honors while she held the glasses.

"Now then," he said, accepting one of them and linking his arm with hers, "this is how it's done in the movies. To us.... May we always be as happy and eager for what the future will bring as we are at this moment."

"To us," Crista echoed, convinced her love for him could fill up the universe.

As they drank, they gazed deeply into each other's eyes. I have a new last name, Crista thought, scarcely able to contain her excitement. Phil is my husband. I'm the luckiest woman in the world.

Then Phil was taking the glass from her fingers and setting it with his beside the hot tub. "Not too much bubbly," he cautioned, his tawny eyes narrowing as he unfastened his tie and tossed it aside. "We want to stay alert enough to appreciate every nuance, every flicker of passion. Don't you think it's time we got undressed?"

Like Crista, he was still wearing his wedding clothes—medium gray slacks, charcoal jacket, a shadow-striped shirt that harmonized with the purple tie he'd selected. As he shrugged off the jacket and began to rid himself of his shirt, her fingers went to her own buttons. Did he want to undress her, too? Or should she...?

The sun had come out again and birds were singing in the coconut palms outside the window. Carrying the tang of salt, a light breeze ruffled the curtains. To Crista it hinted at paradise, finally within her grasp.

"Let's take off our own things while we undress each other with our eyes," Phil suggested, answering her unspoken question.

The erotic proposal sent shivers of need racing to the deep, as yet unfathomed place where she wanted him most. It had the effect of exaggerating her longing, even while it postponed the first moment of gratification. Slowly, allowing herself to linger over every fastening, she removed her shoes, jacket and skirt. Like some besotted gourmand she feasted her eyes on his bare torso and the long, muscular legs revealed as he removed his trousers.

Phil caught his breath when she peeled off her nylons and discarded her bra. He was forced to call every ounce of willpower he possessed into play to keep from reaching out to learn the shape of her breasts with his fingertips.

At last they faced each other, naked except for his boxer shorts and the thin, lace-trimmed wisp of her bikini panties. Their breathing increasingly ragged with anticipation, they shed even those last barriers. Phil's generous male attributes sprang free. She wanted to cradle them in her hands.

Only when they'd fully satisfied their visual hunger did he enfold her. As she pressed tightly against his so-loved body, Crista's feelings of inadequacy melted away. Her tongue was as lusty, as vigorous as his when they claimed each other's mouths.

Both realized their kiss was just the first movement in a dance that held fusion as its aim—one step in an urgent pas de deux that would carry them toward the consummation they craved. With a stifled groan, Phil drew back and led her to the hot tub as he'd planned. But he knew they wouldn't be able to stay there for long.

It had been his intention to frolic with Crista in the tub's inviting ambience, drawing out the preliminaries for as long as possible. Now he acknowledged he might not be able to, their first time together.

The moment they lowered themselves into the seething bubbles, he pulled her back into his arms. They were kneeling together so that his hard expectancy was thrust between her legs. He began to kiss her all over—hair, eyes, mouth, neck—then bent to maraud the sweetly upturned peaks of her rose-and-cream breasts.

Clasping his dark head to her plundered fullness, Crista thought she'd never known a pleasure so carnal yet so achingly tender. She quickly realized she hadn't experienced anything yet. A wordless gasp of delight escaped her when his roving fingers invaded the cleft of her femininity to find the hidden apex of her desire.

All the quivering warmth she'd felt, all her intense longing, seemed to merge and coalesce in a single point of need. Breakers of feeling washed over her, each sharper and more overpowering than the last. Driven by instincts as old as womankind, she arched her back and thrust her lower body forward to meet his touch.

Little cries of astonishment shook her delicate frame as a swell more imperious than any of its predecessors crested and carried her away. Her eyes shut, her head thrown back, she dissolved in wave after wave of rapturous shudders. Gooseflesh shimmered like a veil over her thighs as a delicious lassitude reached to the very soles of her feet. A flush that shamed the water's heat spread over her cheeks.

Deeply affected by the wanton innocence of her response, Phil was racked by his need for her. But Crista's satisfaction, her firsthand discovery of what sex was all about, were too precious for him to diminish with any crude demands. Instead of moving to take his own pleasure, he held himself motionless, absorbing her ripples of ecstasy as if they were his own.

"That's it, baby," he encouraged softly. "Let the feeling take you. Ride it out to the end."

Gradually she quieted, her slender fingers relaxing their grip on his shoulders. With a little sigh, she slumped against him. Only then did he allow himself the luxury of running his hands down the wet curves of her body.

Tentative as the gesture was, it awakened her to the reality of what hadn't happened between them. Thinking only of ensuring her euphoria, Phil had cheated himself of his own.

"Darling..." she began, her voice husky from what she'd just experienced. "You didn't..."

"Hush, I know." Phil placed one finger lightly against her lips. "Was it... all right for you?"

Her lashes were still wet from the tears that had crowded against them. "It was wonderful," she whispered. "I've never felt so alive, yet so completely lost to myself."

He glowed with pride at the implied compliment. "That's exactly how it's supposed to feel," he said.

"But I want you inside me."

It was what he wanted, too. Lovingly he helped her to her feet and guided her to the bed. Crista lay back against the fresh white sheets and pillowcases, inviting him to take her. He paused to savor her nakedness with a smoky look in his eyes as he applied protection. The hard, muscled texture of his masculine flesh contrasted deliciously with her soft, feminine curves as he covered her body.

She was finally going to get her wish. A thrill of anticipation seized her as he nudged at the threshold of her womanhood. Then he was inside, taking possession of the tabernacle no man had claimed before him, owning the secret treasure she'd kept inviolate for his sake.

Sweet Crista, he thought, half wild at the splendor of what he felt. You're mine and only mine. I wish I could have given you such a gift. But he could worship her with his experience, sing her praises from the pinnacle of his need.

Pain flickered briefly in her eyes, though he tried not to hurt her as they came together. But it was nothing beside the exultation Crista felt. In a way she welcomed the slight discomfort as a kind of apotheosis. Like some Olympic runner beset by hardship along the way, she had carried her torch to its destination. Everything she had, everything she was as a woman, now belonged to the man she loved.

I'm home at last, she thought as she cradled him between her thighs. We'll have each other for the rest of our days.

Thoroughly undone by his own selflessness, Phil couldn't wait. But Crista was secure in the knowledge that they'd make love again and again. As she gloried in his shattering culmination, a deep, implosive excitement rose within her and then subsided. She realized she'd almost climaxed again.

Maybe next time I will, she thought lazily as they lay side by side with her head on his shoulder. There's a lot more to lovemaking than I ever dreamed.

For a while they slept, waking to indulge themselves a third time as the setting sun flung its pyrotechnics into the sky. Achieving the deeper fulfillment that had eluded her earlier, Crista felt cherished to the marrow of her being. I'll never get enough of him, she realized.

Teasing and childlike in their playfulness, they showered, luxuriating in the sting of the lukewarm spray against their passion-spent bodies. Then, putting on T-shirts and shorts, they walked barefoot along the shore before cooking themselves a pair of filets on Nick's outdoor grill. Usually a light eater, Crista was ravenous from so much lovemaking.

"I never thought contentment could be so deep," she confessed later, as they star-gazed from canvas chairs on their absent host's patio. The new, exquisitely private memories that connected her with Phil had brought a sublime peace to her soul.

In the morning, Crista had one or two uneasy thoughts. Some evil spirit caused her to remember the exact words they'd spoken just before Phil had asked her to marry him. *I love you so much!* she'd exclaimed, wounded at the thought that he would refuse her again. *I think I feel the same way about you,* he'd replied. Against her will she began to dissect his answer, dredge up the rest of their conversation. He'd never actually spoken the fateful words.

Yet, for one who'd balked at marriage for so long, Phil seemed remarkably content. He patted her fanny affectionately and kissed her several times as they breakfasted and set Nick's house to rights. When they'd finished, like a belated wedding present he divulged that there was rumored to be a nude beach at the easternmost tip of the island. "If there's nobody about, I'll make love to you on the sand and again in the water," he promised. "Or half in, half out, if you prefer."

They arrived to find they had the beach all to themselves. Phil parked the minijeep where it wouldn't be noticed from the road. Stripping down to their swimsuits and then discarding them altogether, they took a quick dip and began making love in the water. Gentle wavelets, leveled by the reef, blended with the crashing breakers of their need.

Swept up in a passion that was mutual and all-consuming, they stumbled ashore for a second culmination.

"I'm wasted, woman," Phil murmured as they stretched out naked on their beach towels atop the powdery sand. "For a novice, you sure know how to please a man."

Though Crista didn't answer, her mouth curved in a secretive little smile. During the past twenty-four hours, she'd only begun to test the extent of her power as a woman. Just wait until I'm *experienced* at this, she told him silently. You're really going to be wasted then.

When they'd recovered sufficiently, Crista suggested they drive into town for lunch. "I'd feel terribly guilty if I didn't wire Gran about the latest developments in my life," she said.

Willing at that point to give her anything she wanted, Phil didn't object. "There's this little café serving Caribbean-style food I've been itching to try, anyway," he replied.

Her telegram duly sent, they strolled to a part of town frequented mostly by St. Croix's native population. On the way there, they stopped at an open-air market on Company Street where Phil sampled several oddities, including tamarind and a brownish fruit with a tough skin and large pit, which the stallkeeper called *mahmee*. To Crista, Phil's choices resembled the kind of produce that might have been available in a prehistoric grocery store. They didn't look like anything *she* would want to eat.

She found the café he'd spotted slightly questionable, as well. A hole-in-the-wall place with bare board floors and oilcloth on the tables, it was patronized exclusively by local residents. There wasn't a tourist in sight, not even on the sidewalk.

Always an adventurous eater, Phil ordered a beer and spicy goat curry with a side dish of *akee*, a prepared vegetable that arrived looking like scrambled eggs. Considering caution to be the better part of valor, Crista settled for a salad and iced, bottled fruit juice.

Though he pronounced his selections delicious, Phil had the beginnings of a stomachache by the time they reached their hotel. His discomfort only got worse as they lay in deck chairs beside the pool trying to make up for lost sleep.

"Maybe you should see a doctor," she ventured, worried by the obvious furrows of pain that creased his forehead.

But Phil wanted nothing to do with her suggestion. "I'll be okay," he insisted with typical stubbornness. "It was that damned goat. Or maybe the *akee*. I never should have eaten them."

Eventually he was forced to compromise. He declared himself willing to drive her into town so she could visit the drugstore on his behalf.

After listening to her tale of woe, the pharmacist sold Crista a purgative to rid Phil's digestive system of whatever was causing the problem. She winced at the man's contention that *akee* could be poisonous if it was picked at the wrong time.

"If this doesn't work, insist your husband see a doctor," the pharmacist advised.

To their dismay, the purgative *did* work—far more effectively than either of them expected. Phil spent most of the night closeted in the bathroom while Crista tried unsuccessfully to sleep. In the morning he was as weak as a newborn lamb, for once lacking in appetite though his stomach cramps were almost gone. They were both groggy from lack of rest.

It was to be their last full day on the island. Resisting the urge to coax him to eat, Crista proposed they spend their morning resting in the shade. Phil's skin had looked a little pink to her following their visit to the nude beach the day before, and he'd steadfastly refused to apply the sun block she used so religiously on herself.

Naturally he wouldn't hear of it. "What I need is to bake this thing out of me," he said, adjusting his chair so that he would absorb the maximum strength of the sun's rays. "Don't forget... we're going back to subzero temperatures and a sky that hunkers down like a gray bowl around your ears. If you'd rather do something else this morning, don't feel you have to baby-sit."

"I thought you liked snow and ice," she retorted. But she couldn't argue with his succinct description of a northern Illinois winter. Reminding herself that no honeymoon was perfect and they'd promised to love each other for better or worse, Crista decided he needed some time to himself. Meanwhile it was her last chance to go snorkeling. She forced herself to bounce back from fatigue and join an expedition from the hotel that had been organized to explore the local reef.

Having been gone all morning and part of the afternoon, she returned with a slight burn despite the preventive measures she'd taken. By contrast, Phil—not having moved from his chair—had ripened to the angry color of a cooked lobster. Gingerly testing his arm as they went upstairs, Crista saw to her dismay that the light pressure of her fingertips left temporary white marks. Oh, no, she thought. Here we go again.

Phil suffered alternately from chills and the furnace flush of his mistreated skin that evening as they ate supper in the hotel dining room. One moment he was radiating heat; the next he was shivering as he caught a draft from the partially open windows.

Sympathetic to his plight even though he'd brought it on himself, Crista resigned herself to another night without lovemaking. I'm a married woman, she thought with a little shake of her head. Yet, at the rate things are going, I'm lucky I managed to hand over my virginity before disaster struck.

She hadn't reckoned on Phil's healthy appetite or masculine pride. I'll be damned if we're going to end up behaving like brother and sister on our honeymoon just because I was stupid enough to get fried in the sun today, he thought. There must be a painless way we can make love to each other.

Glancing in the bathroom mirror, he saw that white squint lines fanned out from his eyes like cracks in parched earth—the alternative to the bandit's mask his sunglasses would have made if he'd been wearing them. His eyes looked a little bloodshot, he decided. As he stood there, his skin seemed to tighten over his cheekbones and go up another notch in temperature.

"Got anything for sunburn?" he asked.

The prudent type, Crista had brought both analgesic creams and a tube of aloe gel. "Lie down and I'll put some stuff on you," she said.

He peeled off his clothes, feeling as if his skin—not simply the fabric of T-shirt and shorts—were being stripped from his body. But the cream felt good and the gel even better; they were cool enough against his skin to make him shiver. Crista's hands were soft, careful and infinitely talented.

When she'd finished, he wanted to go to sleep. But he also wanted to make love to her. "Do you think...you could be careful not to touch me in too many places?" he asked.

Crista did her best. But *almost* everywhere their bodies brushed brought Phil pain as well as pleasure. She had smeared a white ointment on his nose and as a result he looked impossibly clownish, making her want to laugh at the most inopportune moments.

Suddenly, "The hell with this," he growled. "We're going to do things right."

Steeling himself to the discomfort of direct contact, he rolled her over and did a swift, thorough job of bringing her to the peak she craved. But his own satisfaction was more than either of them could orchestrate. Even the gentlest caress on Crista's part was torture too keen to bear. To make matters worse, both of them were slippery from all the glop she'd applied to him.

"Tomorrow's another day," he said at last, giving up with a sigh and stretching out against the sheets.

Sorry she hadn't been able to bring him to release, Crista was fully content herself. She wanted only to shut her eyes and venture into dreamland. Taking care not to cause him any more anguish than necessary, she kissed him goodnight.

Tossing and turning in his effort to find a semblance of comfort, Phil got up at some point after midnight and switched on the television set. Crista found herself dozing fitfully as she tried to ignore his complaints about the dearth of local programming and regular bulletins on the state of his sunburn.

Finally she'd had enough. Sitting up in bed, she uttered the first cross words of their marriage. "Would you *please* try not to talk while I'm asleep?" she asked.

Chapter Twelve

They were both exhausted and cranky the next morning as they stood in line at customs, inching their luggage forward with their feet. No sooner had they reached the departure gate than an unsettling announcement crackled over the public address system. Due to a computer breakdown on St. Thomas, seat assignments already given out couldn't be guaranteed, the unseen speaker advised. It was likely there had been some duplication. "Please take the first available seat," he requested.

A mad scramble of passengers up the boarding steps ending in their having to sit apart. Phil found himself in the plane's center section surrounded by several families with restless youngsters. Sliding into an empty seat beside a dour businessman several rows forward, Crista thankfully took two aspirin for her headache and went to sleep.

Miami was as noisy and frenetic as it had been on their southbound journey. Though they managed to get adjoining seats on their connecting flight, they didn't seem to have much to talk about. Phil's sunburn was still bothering him, while Crista continued to long for uninterrupted rest.

They landed in Chicago nearly an hour late. During their absence, a Canadian cold front had sagged over the city, validating Phil's prediction of subzero temperatures. As they struggled to collect their luggage in the usual crush, someone called out Phil's name in surprise.

Shaken out of their lethargy, he and Crista turned to face a stacked, self-assured blonde in tan safari-type clothing. The blonde was accompanied by a swarthy, sardonic-looking male whose shoulders were hung about with expensive camera equipment. Crista didn't recognize her, though she had to admit the man looked very familiar. Her eyes widened when the blonde put her arms around Phil's neck and kissed him on the mouth.

To his credit, Phil recoiled in embarrassment. He couldn't believe his rotten luck. By some horrible coincidence, they'd bumped into Irene Maher, his erstwhile fiancée, and Pepe Romero, his photographer roommate, less than twenty minutes after arriving in Chicago.

"Irene... Pepe..." he acknowledged weakly. "What are you doing here?"

"We've just arrived home from Central America," Irene replied, giving Crista an appraising look. "I might ask you the same question."

"We...uh, just got in from St. Croix."

There was a small silence. "Aren't you going to introduce us to your friend?" Irene asked.

Phil looked as if he'd rather be hung than perform such a task. But he couldn't think of any reason to refuse. "Irene, Pepe, I want you to meet Crista O'Malley," he complied. "Crista, Pepe is my roommate. He and Irene both work at the paper."

Crista's stomach did a flip-flop at his words. He'd used her maiden name instead of her married one! Wasn't he proud of her? Didn't he want people to realize they were man and wife?

"I'm happy to meet you both," she said in a small voice.

Pepe gave her an engaging grin. "My pleasure," he answered, giving her figure a practiced once-over.

Irene's response was a bit more formal and decidedly chillier. "How do you do?" she said, raising one eyebrow at Phil. "You work at the paper, too, don't you, Crista?"

"Yes. I'm relatively new there."

"I thought so. Why don't we all share a cab into town?"

Managing a moment alone with Crista while Pepe hailed them a taxi and Irene went in search of a missing bag, Phil confessed the awful truth. He and Irene had been engaged before she'd left on assignment with his roommate three-and-a-half months earlier.

"I swear it was nothing serious," he apologized, not realizing how irresponsible it made him sound. "I never planned to marry her. But as a gentleman I need time to explain myself. Would you hate me too much if we dropped you off at your place? I should take her out for coffee or something."

It was hardly the ecstatic homecoming Crista had pictured the day of their wedding in Christiansted. She was extremely reluctant to hand her new husband over to another woman, even on a temporary basis. But she didn't want to start out their marriage by evincing a lack of trust. At least he'd given her a satisfactory reason for not making the proper introductions.

"No, I wouldn't hate you," Crista said.

He gave her an abjectly grateful look. "I'll call you just as soon as I can," he promised.

Come by and *get* me just as soon as you can, she wanted to answer. But she didn't dare put her request into words. Pepe and Irene were back within earshot.

Things were awkward in the cab, and in a way, Crista was relieved to be dropped off first. She felt completely disoriented as she let herself into the apartment she shared with Laurin Hayes. Were her marriage to Phil and the blissful lovemaking she remembered at Nick's house and the nude beach merely figments of her imagination? Or had they actually taken place?

It was just her luck that her roommate was home. Rabidly curious, Laurin pounced, demanding an instant recounting of Crista's adventures. "I want to hear absolutely *everything*!" she insisted, dragging Crista to the sofa for a thorough gabfest. "Did you go through with it? How do you like sex?"

Crista didn't answer. The expression on her face made Laurin hesitate. Then Crista's roommate spied the emerald wedding set on Crista's left hand and gave a little shriek.

"You're...married?" Laurin asked incredulously, holding Crista's hand with its sparkling new rings up to the light. "I don't believe it! Why don't you look happier? And who's the lucky guy?"

Having learned from Dan that Phil had followed Crista to St. Croix, Laurin wasn't too surprised to learn that he was the bridegroom. "I knew you'd eventually convince him bachelorhood was for the birds." She laughed. "Where *is* that handsome devil, anyway? Why isn't he with you? I want to congratulate him!"

Laurin's brows drew together as Crista reluctantly described what had taken place at the airport. "Irene Maher!" she exclaimed, wildly partisan on Crista's behalf. "I never could figure out what he saw in her. Don't feel bad, honey. The whole thing between the two of you was kind of sudden. Phil will get used to it. Everything's going to be all right."

Crista wasn't so certain. Laurin's hasty assurances only strengthened her own feeling that more than a leftover fiancée stood between her and happiness. Like it or not, the worries she'd entertained the first morning of her marriage had cropped up again. She wondered if Phil was sorry he'd proposed to her. Though they'd been married more than seventy-two hours, he still hadn't mentioned the word *love*.

As they unloaded their luggage at the apartment he and Pepe shared, Phil noticed his roommate removing Irene's bags from the taxi, too. But he didn't attach much significance to the gesture. No doubt Pepe thought Irene would be staying over with him as she had occasionally in the past. Boy, would he be surprised when he found out the truth!

Eager to get through the unpleasant business of breaking the news to Irene as quickly as possible, Phil suggested they stash her things directly in the trunk of his car. "I'll drive you home," he offered.

Pepe and Irene gave each other a look. "All right," she agreed in a speculative tone.

Phil's thoughts were churning as they drove off in the general direction of her building. I feel like such a heel, he told himself—even if I never believed she took me seriously, either. "Let's go out for a hamburger or something," he proposed, realizing that neither of them had broken the silence since they'd gotten in the car together. "I have to talk to you."

"Ditto," said Irene, crossing her legs.

The place they chose wasn't fancy but it produced great burgers. Phil hardly tasted his. A spurt of catsup dribbled on his chin when his former fiancée announced that in the jungles of Central America, she and Pepe had become more than a professional team.

"Being engaged to you was great fun while it lasted," she said, obviously relishing his astonishment. "But I don't think anything ever would have come of it. With Pepe, I've finally found what I've been looking for. Now...don't you have something to explain about that girl you were with at the airport?"

Immensely relieved, though his pride had been nicked, Phil was about to answer when he was gripped by a hearty sneeze. Suddenly his eyes were itching and one side of his nose was completely stuffed. Though he was almost never sick, he realized he was suffering from an instant head cold in addition to his sunburn. His barely settled stomach was also objecting to the burger he'd consumed.

To make matters worse, Irene informed him she planned to spend the night with Pepe at Phil's former apartment. No way can I bring Crista there now, he thought. Or even hang around myself. Yet, rotten as he felt, he was longing for a familiar bed. But he didn't want to stay at Crista's place with Dan and Laurin underfoot, asking a billion questions.

The truth was, now that the honeymoon was over, he didn't know quite how to settle into this marriage thing.

What he needed was comforting surroundings, someone serene and wise to take care of him who hadn't been robbed of sleep for two nights running and wasn't directly involved in his mixed-up situation. I know, he decided, dropping Irene and her luggage off at the Lake Shore Drive place. I'll go home to Melrose Park. Mama will know what to do.

As Phil expected, Luisa Catterini welcomed him with open arms. "*Caro*, you're sick! I think you have a fever," she remonstrated, stepping back to lay the inside of her wrist gently against his forehead. "And a sunburn in January... Only you would turn up with that!"

Quickly she provided Phil with cold medication, a steaming mug of hot tea with lemon and honey stirred into it, and a pair of his father's pajamas. Soon he was installed in his old room with several blankets pulled up to his chin. He knew he should tell his mother about his marriage to Crista, but it felt so good to be petted and cared-for after so many mishaps that he couldn't bring himself to say a word.

Something about the way his mother fussed over him hinted she'd guessed his problems weren't just physical. "Get some sleep, son," she admonished, kissing him and switching off the lamp. "We'll talk tomorrow, after you've had some rest."

The tea and cold medication beginning to lull his awareness, Phil wanted nothing more than to take her advice. But before he could shut his eyes, he had a promise to keep. He guessed Crista would be furious with him for leaving her alone at her old apartment and taking refuge at his parents' place. He'd just have to face up to that.

"Where *are* you?" she asked plaintively when he slipped downstairs to give her a call. "You can't still be drinking coffee with your former fiancée."

"No, I'm out in Melrose Park," he answered. "I told Irene about us. She's engaged to Pepe now, so she didn't mind a bit. But they're staying at our... that is, my former apartment. So we can hardly go there."

Well, are you coming here? she demanded—though she didn't phrase the question aloud. When am I going to see you? she wondered.

"I decided to drive out and tell my folks about us," he explained semitruthfully into the silent receiver. "As you can probably tell, I've come down with a terrible cold. My mother gave me something for it and I'm too sleepy now to drive. If you don't mind, I'll just stay here tonight."

Stunned, Crista didn't know what to say.

"Tomorrow's Sunday," he added to placate her. "We can start looking for an apartment then."

For a moment he thought she'd lost her capacity for speech. Then, "What did your parents say about our getting married?" Crista asked.

Something made her hold her breath as she waited for his answer. "I didn't tell them yet," Phil admitted after a slight pause. "But I will...just as soon as I get a chance."

That night, Crista cried herself to sleep. He doesn't love me, she thought. Our marriage was a lifetime commitment for me and a spontaneous lark for Phil. He's already regretting it. What am I going to do?

She was extremely quiet and withdrawn when he picked her up the next day. Though they scanned every inch of the classifieds and visited a number of apartments, the ones they looked at were either crummy, too far from work or too expensive, even with their combined salaries. Dejected, they shared a pizza at a local eatery although neither of them had much appetite. It was a terrible way to start a marriage.

"I guess it's a hotel for us tonight," Phil remarked glumly, popping an antihistamine tablet before paying the bill. "Or your apartment, if that's okay with Laurin."

"I'm sure it would be fine with her if we stayed there," Crista replied.

That night, they didn't make love. Kissing each other like polite strangers, they settled down to sleep in the twin beds in Crista's room. It felt as if they were a million miles apart. Though she'd wanted to ask him at least a dozen times, Crista still didn't know if Phil had told the elder Catterinis about their marriage. She guessed he probably hadn't. Meanwhile she hadn't even called her grandmother. I don't want Gran to worry unless it's absolutely necessary, she thought. But things are getting to that point.

When they awoke to a chilly gray dawn, Phil informed her that he had to go back to his old place for a change of clothing. "I might as well shower there," he mumbled. "Guess I'll see you at the office. I might have to work late today. I've got a column to write."

After he'd gone, Crista sat down on the edge of her bed and buried her face in her hands. You have to think, she told herself shakily. And Phil needs time—time by himself—to decide whether or not he wants to go ahead with our marriage. You can't push. This is something he has to figure out all by himself.

Deciding on a course of action, she went to the phone. It wasn't easy, but she made herself dial Harry Jenkins's number at the paper.

"Harry," she said when he came on the line, "I need a big favor, no questions asked."

"Shoot," he replied in his unruffled fashion.

"A couple more days off," she pleaded. "I know.... I just got back from vacation. But this is an emergency. You might say it's a matter of the heart."

Though he grumbled, Harry gave Crista her wish. In the apartment's other bedroom, Laurin was still fast asleep. Quickly throwing some comfort clothes into an overnight bag, Crista scribbled a note to her friend. "If Phil calls, tell him I've gone away for a few days to think things over. And please don't worry about me. I'll be all right."

Having called a cab, she was soon on her way to Wilmette. Her grandmother greeted her with a fond hug.

"Crista, my dear child!" she exclaimed. "It's so good to see you. When I got your telegram..."

Slowly Mary Rose Burke's voice trailed off as she took in the small suitcase and the tearful expression on Crista's face. "Come in by the fire and tell me about it, darling," she soothed, her sprightly blue eyes brimming with sympathy. "I'll have Essie make you a nice cup of hot chocolate. When a person's upset, chocolate's wonderful for the soul."

Gently Crista's grandmother elicited the whole sorry tale, including Crista's plan to shed her virginity with some willing stranger if that was what it took to get the man she wanted. To Crista's surprise, Mary Rose Burke wasn't angry or judgmental, though she agreed it had been a foolhardy scheme.

"I was madly in love once upon a time myself," she reminisced. "Your grandfather was a fetching rogue, and I thought the sun rose and set on him. I would have done almost anything to keep him. In my opinion, Philip Catterini is a very intelligent and deserving young man. He's just wriggling a little on the hook, that's all. If I were you, I'd lie low for a few days... give him ample opportunity to think things over and realize what a splendid young woman he's married to."

"Oh, Gran..." Crista threw her arms around Mary Rose's neck and began to weep. "I keep feeling as if I took advantage of Phil at a vulnerable moment! But what was I supposed to do? Say *no* when the man I love asked me to marry him?"

Her grandmother patted her as reassuringly as if she were a child. "No woman in her right mind would have done such a thing," she said.

* * *

In his corner of the *Tribune*'s feature department, Phil was deep into a column about the hazards of travel to tropical climes. It was a kind of catharsis for him, and he found he was feeling much better both physically and mentally. What an ass I've been, he admitted to himself, pausing for a sip of the bitter-tasting coffee one of his fellow staffers had made. Crista is a marvel and I love her—more than I ever knew it was possible to love anyone. Though the circumstances were pretty unorthodox, I'm *glad* we got married when we did.

At the same time, he realized Crista might not know how he felt. Suddenly he was aching to tell her. To his mounting frustration, the morning passed and then a good part of the afternoon without Crista putting in an appearance at her desk in the news department. She hadn't mentioned anything about having to cover a lengthy trial, though of course they'd talked mostly about apartments and his head cold the day before.

Maybe she wasn't feeling well. Had she caught his cold and decided to stay home in bed? But there wasn't any answer when he phoned her apartment. Finally he walked over to Harry Jenkins's desk. "Wasn't Crista O'Malley supposed to be back from vacation today?" he asked.

Busy editing copy, Harry barely glanced in his direction. "Yeah," he replied. "She called in for an extension."

For a moment Phil brightened, figuring she'd gone apartment hunting on her own. Instinct told him he was mistaken. On a hunch, he called her grandmother's house.

"I'm sorry, Philip," Mary Rose Burke told him in a faintly reproving tone. "But I'm not at liberty to discuss Crista's whereabouts."

Say what he would, he couldn't change the older woman's mind. I can't believe it, he thought, putting down the receiver. But Crista has left me. A few minutes later, Laurin arrived at the office to begin her afternoon shift and confirmed his worst fears. His imagination running riot, he pictured himself and Crista in divorce court.

No! he told himself fiercely. I won't let that happen! With a start, he realized how desperately he longed for what had been anathema to him such a short time before: marriage, a home and children—a whole tribe of them, if that's what Crista wanted. Frantic to tell her so and fearful she wanted nothing more to do with him, he finished off the column in a burst of clumsy prose. Half an hour later, he was brooding in circles as he walked along Michigan Avenue, muffled against the bitter chill.

Evening found Crista wrapped in a soft old quilt, listening to Strauss waltzes and playing checkers with her grandmother before the fire.

Meanwhile Phil had turned up on his parents' doorstep again. This time he confessed everything, as he and his mother had coffee at the breakfast-nook table.

Luisa Catterini listened with growing amazement to his tale of the past week's events. Though she shook her head several times, a little smile began to play about the corners of her mouth.

"Thank goodness you've finally settled down...and with such a lovely girl," she said when he had finished. "But you're right, son. You've behaved like a complete idiot. Crista is one in a million, a precious commodity in today's easy-come, easy-go world. You can't afford to let her get away."

Phil groaned. "Do you think I don't know that?" he asked impatiently. "What am I going to do?"

"I'm not sure if there's anything you *can* do immediately," his mother admitted after a moment's thought. "I have a feeling that even if Crista is staying with her grandmother, Mrs. Burke won't allow you to see her for the next few days. But all's not lost unless you're willing that should be the case. From what I can tell, Crista is truly in love with you. Put that brilliant head of yours to work and come up with a creative way of letting her know where you stand."

For several minutes, Phil stared blankly at his coffee cup. A billboard would cost him a fortune and he had no guarantee she'd see it, anyway. A skywriter would be perfect—impress her with his dramatic flair. But it posed the same problems. Plus the technique wouldn't work to good effect against Chicago's wintry overcast. What then? he asked himself.

"I know!" he suddenly exclaimed, getting to his feet. "Thanks, Mama! You're a gem!"

Racing out the door, he drove at top speed back to the paper. "Kill that trash I wrote this afternoon," he begged his astonished editor. "I've got a better idea. I promise I'll have it ready in time for the first edition!"

Like a man possessed, he sat down at his computer and poured on the steam. Forty-five minutes later, he'd finished and sent his copy to the editor's desk. A snappy, graying woman in her early fifties, she read it and came over to talk to him.

"You're right. The stuff you wrote earlier was trash," she said, giving him an appraising look. "Your current effort is much better. But I have to admit it's a bit unorthodox."

"You're going to run it anyway, aren't you?" Phil asked, feeling as if his future hung on her reply.

"Yeah, we'll run it," she conceded with a smile. "This time it really must be love."

Crista woke up the next morning determined not to let Phil ruin her life. Instead of hiding out at her grandmother's house, she decided to get dressed and go back to work. *I was lucky enough to be hired by one of the top ten newspapers in the country,* she thought, dialing Harry's number. *And I want to keep my job—even if Phil and I are history. Somehow, I'll have to tough it out.*

Yet, despite her show of bravery, she couldn't bear to read the column her husband had written the night before. Though she brought in Mary Rose's *Trib* from the front porch, she didn't even remove it from its protective wrapper.

For the first time in her career, Crista arrived at the courthouse to make her rounds without having scanned the morning paper. To her consternation, everywhere she went, people asked her if she'd seen that day's edition of "Catbird Seat."

"No, I haven't," she was forced to admit, over and over until she wanted to scream.

"Maybe you'd better have a look at it, Crista," one of the judges advised in a kindly tone.

All the important hearings she'd been planning to cover had been postponed, anyway. Taking the elevator back down to the lobby, Crista inserted a quarter into one of the newspaper boxes and pulled out a copy of that day's *Trib*. Sitting down on one of the benches, she turned with trembling fingers to Phil's column. *This morning,* he began, *I'm hanging from the Catbird Seat by a thread....*

To her chagrin, embarrassment and finally her unmitigated delight, Crista dwelt on his every word as he exposed her as "Kate," described all but their most intimate adventures and broadcast the news of their marriage to the world.

Like most confirmed bachelors, I didn't know a good thing when I saw it. I didn't realize I had the best, the sweetest, the most wonderful wife a man could want. And so I forgot to tell her that I love her very much.

If you see her today in your travels about the city, please ask her if she's read this message. Once she does, I'm hoping she'll give me a call.

Tears running down her cheeks, Crista ran to the nearest pay phone and dialed Phil's work number. He answered on the first ring.

"Is this the *Tribune*'s consumer help line?" she asked pertly. "If so, I've got a problem. I have a marriage document here that guarantees me love, sex and a warm body next to me in bed at night. For the past few days, I haven't been getting any of the above. Do you think you can help?"

"*Can* I?"

Phil's voice was ecstatic. "Just tell me where you are and I'll be right over!"

Figuratively floating on air, Crista laughed with the bubbly sound that so enchanted him. "We can't make love at the courthouse!" she protested.

"That's what you think," he replied. "However, we won't have to. In the hope that you might give me another chance, I've reserved a suite for us at the Palmer House."

Crista felt cosseted, treasured and loved to distraction as Phil led her beneath the tan-and-gold marquee of one of Chicago's premier hotels. The lobby's elegant rose-and-green patterned carpet, its lavish use of candelabra, gold leaf and marble—even the dignified bustle of the smartly uniformed bellhops—hinted that rooms there would be expensive. She didn't dare ask what a *suite* had cost.

Twenty minutes later, she and Phil were nestled between the sheets of a king-size French provincial bed. Crystal lamps graced the matching night tables. An armoire hid a TV and an FM radio. For the night, at least, they were the proud possessors of a vast living-and-dining space appointed with apricot print furnishings and a berry-colored carpet. A special "refreshment center" containing everything from ice, Scotch and fruit juice to foie-gras pâté and cookies awaited their pleasure.

They were too busy to think about anything but each other. "Did you really mean it when you wrote you hoped we could buy a house in the suburbs and have children together?" Crista asked.

"I did," he confirmed. "Shut up and kiss me."

It was exactly what she wanted to do. Though they'd have a lifetime to love and cherish each other, they both wanted to put the anguish of the past few days behind them as quickly as possible.

On her mouth, Phil's was hungry and insistent. His tongue probed with the greed of a pirate delving deep into a hard-won treasure. With little stabs of longing she began to anticipate the even deeper union that would unite them in just moments.

She gave a soft little cry as his mouth trailed down to her breasts and then sought the protected nest of her femininity to tease her into readiness. They wouldn't reach for glory separately this time. He knew without having to be told that she wanted him inside.

Pulsing in her most private places, his fullness pushed her past reason. It wasn't long before she was spinning out of control, attaining new summits of rapture. Suddenly she dissolved in an explosion of fireworks that set him ablaze. Seconds later, Phil followed, fusing them with his shudders of ecstasy.

We're joined so profoundly, so completely, nothing can ever separate us, Crista thought as she drifted back down like an ember in his arms. Our marriage isn't just a piece of paper any longer. It's a loving contract of the heart.

"I'm so happy," she whispered when they quieted. "I must be the happiest woman in the world."

"Then I'm the happiest man." Phil felt more relaxed and at peace than he could remember. "I've got a surprise for you, sweetheart. Or rather, a couple of surprises. My brother Joe knows somebody who knows somebody who wants to sublet a great Lake Shore Drive apartment. It's partly furnished and the price is right. The owners had to leave for Paris unexpectedly. It'll be available this weekend."

The prospect of a place of their own sounded like sheer heaven after what they'd been through. But Phil had taught Crista she could have everything. "That's marvelous," she answered, kissing him. "I know I'm going to love it. What's the other surprise you were talking about?"

He shrugged, attempting to draw out the suspense. "Nothing much," he hedged. "I talked to my editor and Harry Jenkins, that's all. They agreed to give us leave next month so we can have a real honeymoon."

Afloat on a sea of contentment, Crista rested her head on his shoulder. "How lovely!" she exclaimed. "Where shall we go? The Virgin Islands again? We could get in some additional snorkeling. Lie out in the sun. Sample some more native food...."

There was a small silence and she could almost feel her new husband adjusting his sights downward from the mountaintop where she knew he'd focused them. "If that's what you want," he answered in a quiet voice.

"It isn't," she replied, loving him more every moment as she tickled him in the ribs. "I'll always think of St. Croix fondly, and I'd love to travel back there someday. But right now I'd rather go someplace snowy—like Colorado—and learn to ski. Besides, there's more incentive to cuddle in a cold climate."

* * * * *

Diamond Jubilee Collection

It's our 10th Anniversary...
and *you* get a present!

This collection of early Silhouette Romances features novels written by three of your favorite authors:

ANN MAJOR—*Wild Lady*
ANNETTE BROADRICK—*Circumstantial Evidence*
DIXIE BROWNING—*Island on the Hill*

* These Silhouette Romance titles were first published in the early 1980s and have not been available since!

* Beautiful Collector's Edition bound in antique green simulated leather to last a lifetime!

* Embossed in gold on the cover and spine!

------------------------------------>✂ **PROOF OF PURCHASE**

This special collection will not be sold in retail stores and is only available through this exclusive offer:

Send your name, address and zip or postal code, along with six proof-of-purchase coupons from any Silhouette Romance published in June, July and/or August, plus $2.50 for postage and handling (check or money order—please do not send cash) payable to Silhouette Reader Service to:

In the U.S.	In Canada
Free Book Offer	Free Book Offer
Silhouette Books	Silhouette Books
901 Fuhrmann Blvd.	P.O. Box 609
Box 9055	Fort Erie, Ontario
Buffalo, NY 14269-9055	L2A 5X3

(Please allow 4-6 weeks for delivery. Hurry! Quantities are limited.
Offer expires September 30, 1990.)

DJC-1A

SILHOUETTE·INTIMATE·MOMENTS®

Premiering in September, a captivating new cover for Silhouette's most adventurous series!

Every month, Silhouette Intimate Moments sweeps you away with four dramatic love stories rich in passion. Silhouette Intimate Moments presents love at its most romantic, where life is exciting and dreams do come true.

Look for the new cover next month, wherever you buy Silhouette® books.

Silhouette Books®

Take 4 bestselling love stories FREE

Plus get a FREE surprise gift!

Special Limited-time Offer

Mail to   **Silhouette Reader Service®**

In the U.S.
901 Fuhrmann Blvd.
P.O. Box 1867
Buffalo, N.Y. 14269-1867

In Canada
P.O. Box 609
Fort Erie, Ontario
L2A 5X3

YES! Please send me 4 free Silhouette Romance® novels and my free surprise gift. Then send me 6 brand-new novels every month, which I will receive months before they appear in bookstores. Bill me at the already low price of $2.25* each. There are no shipping, handling or other hidden costs. I understand that accepting these books and gifts places me under no obligation ever to buy any books. I can always return a shipment and cancel at any time. Even if I never buy another book from Silhouette, the 4 free books and the surprise gift are mine to keep forever.

* Offer slightly different in Canada—$2.25 per book plus 69¢ per shipment for delivery.

Sales tax applicable in N.Y. and Iowa.

215 BPA HAYY (US)   315 BPA 8176 (CAN)

Name _____ (PLEASE PRINT)

Address _____ Apt. No. _____

City _____ State/Prov. _____ Zip/Postal Code _____

This offer is limited to one order per household and not valid to present Silhouette Romance® subscribers. Terms and prices are subject to change.

© 1990 Harlequin Enterprises Limited

COMING SOON...

For years Harlequin and Silhouette novels have been taking readers places—but only in their imaginations.

This fall look for PASSPORT TO ROMANCE, a promotion that could take you around the corner or around the world!

Watch for it in September!

★

Harlequin® / Silhouette®